THE HAUNTINGS BACK HOME

Rebecca Cuthbert

UNDERTAKER BOOKS

THE HAUNTINGS BACK HOME

By Rebecca Cuthbert

Poem by Beatrice Sheehan

Foreword and Thirteenth Story by Jonathan Gensler

UNDERTAKER BOOKS
www.undertakerbooks.com

CONTENTS

Praise for THE HAUNTINGS BACK HOME — IX

Dedication — XIII

Additional Titles by — XV
Rebecca Cuthbert

First Publication Credits — XVII

Foreword — XIX

When You Wander in the Woods — 1
by Beatrice Sheehan

1. Downstairs at The Sabine — 4
   (The night watchman of a decrepit hotel discovers
   what's hiding in the bowels of the grand building)

2. The One That Got Away — 21
   (An isolated Canadian town is haunted by a decades-old
   danger)

3. Ghost in the Gas Station Bathroom — 38
   (A third-shift clerk dreads cleaning the men's room, for
   good reason)

4. The Vines That Bind   43
    (A woman takes on her dead mother-in-law—and loses)

5. Let the Black Dog In   57
    (Sooner or later, a woman must mourn)

6. Suffer with the Trees   59
    (A lonely newlywed learns that nature does not forgive
    and does not forget)

7. Ghost-Knocking   77
    (Mischievous boys find out payback is a bitch)

8. Mrs. Anderson, Mrs. Anderson   79
    (The homecare nurse of a dying woman takes too soon
    what can never truly be hers)

9. The Hole Had Always Been There   93
    (A grieving teenager must decide whether he'll follow
    his dead mother into darkness or stay topside with his
    hopeless father)

10. Dead Man's Pie   101
    (Just because a stolen pie was eaten doesn't mean it can't
    be taken back)

11. Restoring the Empire Review   103
    (A reserved historian tries to cover up a theater's bawdy
    past, but those who remain refuse to be shamed)

12. Rock-a-Bye   117
    (A bereft would-be mother with a probably straying
    husband finds solace in a forgotten cemetery grove)

13. One Red Glove   136
       by Jonathan Gensler

Thank You   141

Acknowledgments   142

About Rebecca Cuthbert   145

About Jonathan Gensler   147

About Beatrice Sheehan   149

Reader Advisories   151

UB Website   153

PRAISE FOR THE HAUNTINGS BACK HOME

"There's no escaping the places that made you, and nobody knows it better than Rebecca Cuthbert. In THE HAUNTINGS BACK HOME, Cuthbert wastes no time in hammering you with the classics: sea-monsters, murder, revenge, and ghosts. The metaphorical ghosts that haunt us all—grief, regret, agony, guilt—but also literal ghosts. A *lot* of ghosts."
—Christopher O'Halloran, author of PUSHING DAISY

"A collection that should adorn the shelves of any fan of horror literature, THE HAUNTINGS BACK HOME is a testament to Cuthbert's mastery of the ghost story."
—Moaner Lawrence, author of "Bad Newes from New England," "The Great American Nightmare," "Beholden," and more.

"Cuthbert has done it again with this surprising and innovative

small-town folk horror collection! THE HAUNTINGS BACK HOME is chock full of wonderfully evocative tales of the ghosts in the bathroom, in an old abandoned pool, or a fjord, plus sex workers' spirits from another time, and persistent first wives and mothers-in-law. I absolutely loved these fresh, creepy tales!"
—Lindsay Merbaum, author of THE GOLD PERSIMMON and VAMPIRES AT SEA

"Thirteen tales, thirteen ghosts—from vengeful spirits to chilling symbols of grief, Cuthbert and Gensler's collection is haunting, clever, and immersive. Standout stories include "The One That Got Away," about an isolated Canadian town where citizens are being hunted by a decades-old danger, "The Vines that Bind," featuring a vindictive mother-in-law's ghost with a fondness for pumpkins, "Let the Black Dog In," a short-but-sweet examination of mourning, and "The Hole Had Always Been There," an equally effective symbolic take on the grieving process."
—Chloe York, author of OUR DEVIL'S AWAKE

"Rebecca Cuthbert's THE HAUNTINGS BACK HOME is not the kind of book you want to read if you're a fan of happy endings. There are none. No, this is a book where the vengeful ghosts win, the monsters get their victim, and the dead don't stay that way for very long. Luckily, I like that kind of thing. Cuthbert has put together a nice collection of twelve hard, dark stories (with a

thirteenth by guest author Jonathan Gensler, who also contributes the foreword). Some are shorter than others, flash fiction really. My favorites were "The One That Got Away," "The Vines that Bind," and "Suffer with the Trees." They hit the hardest, but you're not going to find a bad one in the bunch. These are nightmares come to life, both for the reader and the poor characters in the stories themselves. Cuthbert takes readers to places where spirits whisper in the night, a footstep or closing door is always a harbinger of danger, and you can't trust the things you see. In short, it's a must-read for anyone who digs a good spine-chilling tale."
—JG Faherty, author of THE MALTHUSIAN CORRECTION, WHEN SEPTEMBER ENDS, and THE WAKENING

"Diversity is the source of biological strength, and this book proves the same is true of stories. Sharp teeth and personified melancholy, inescapable landscapes and relationships. THE HAUNTINGS BACK HOME will stalk your dreams."
—Liam Burke, Silver Tier author of STEPS ON THE PATH

"These stories are dangerous stories, the kind that pull you in and then drag you under before you know what's happening. Sharp, deadly, and beautiful, they run the gamut from ghosts to monsters and more, all the while keeping you ensnared and at their mercy."

—Paul Jessup, author of SKINLESS MAN COUNTS TO FIVE and GLASS HOUSE

"With each story, Cuthbert knows just how to lure you in and plunge you into the depths of grief, loneliness, and horror. You'll be gasping for breath until the last page. It's an absolute must-read."

—Aimee Hardy, author of POCKET FULL OF TEETH

This collection of hauntings is dedicated to the Anderson-Lee Library in Silver Creek, NY, where I first fell in love with ghost stories (and with the smell of old books).

ADDITIONAL TITLES BY
Rebecca Cuthbert

In Memory of Exoskeletons
(poetry, Alien Buddha Press)

CREEP THIS WAY: How to Become a Horror Writer with 24 Tips to Get You Ghouling
(nonfiction, Seamus & Nunzio Productions)

Self-Made Monsters
(poetry and stories, Alien Buddha Press and Undertaker Books)

Down in the Dark Deep Where the Puddlers Dwell
(all-ages picture book, AEA Press and Malediction)

Six O'Clock House & Other Strange Tales
(stories, Watertower Hill Publishing)

FIRST PUBLICATION CREDITS

The following stories were published in these magazines and anthologies, or performed on these podcasts, in current or earlier forms:

"Ghost in the Gas Station Bathroom" was included in *Tales of Sley House 2024* and performed on the *Sley House Presents* podcast by Sley House Publishing

"The Vines That Bind" was performed on the *NoSleep Podcast*

"Ghost Knocking" was included in *Nom Nom: Halowe'en Dark Drabbles* by Black Hare Press

"Mrs. Anderson, Mrs. Anderson" was included in *Two for the Show* by Rebellion LIT

"The Hole Had Always Been There" was included in *Between Doorways* by Salt Heart Press

"Dead Man's Pie" was included in *Cursed Cooking: A Horror Community Cookbook and Food Horror Anthology* by Cat Eye Press

"Restoring the Empire Review" was included in *The Horror Zine*, Spring 2025

"Rock-a-Bye" was included in *Dead Avenue Vol. 2* by Reader2Writer Press

FOREWORD

There's heartbreak here, and despair

and

there's murder here, and rage and blood and the smallest sliver of a knife wielded by your own ghost.

The freshly peeled skin of a life gone wrong is here. There's crime and violence and the quiet, whispering solace of a child's grave, footprints caught in mud made of a would-be mother's unceasing tears.

The voice in your head will be Rebecca Cuthbert's.

Presumably you already know that, or you wouldn't be reading this already-too-long foreword, but please, lend me your patience for just another moment or two.

I met my dear friend Rebecca in the early summer of 2022 in Denver at the annual gathering of horror writers, editors, and publishers know as StokerCon. It was the first StokerCon for both of us, and if she was as nervous as I about going to a convention with around 500 new, unknown people, she didn't show it. She graciously introduced me to the group she was with, and we bonded initially over our shared history with the state of West

Virginia, where Rebecca earned her MFA, and I was born and raised.

(A quick aside – why do the misty green hillsides of West Virginia produce such an abundance of writers of dark, horrific fiction? I have some theories and am happy to talk your ear off about them should we ever cross paths.)

Over the course of the next several months, we began sharing stories with one another, joining several workshops together, and getting to peer into the depths of each other's words. And now, for the last few years, we have spent an hour or so each week together writing, writing, writing. And sharing, sharing, sharing. Her voice grows sharper, the themes she revisits more poignant, and the confidence with which she wields her knife ever more wry. Rebecca is no killer, but she will lure you into a sublimely set trap and let you do the damage to yourself, all while weeding her garden or canning tomatoes for the winter that will certainly blow in any day. She'll hand you the knife, fresh off the sharpening stone, knowing very well that what you do with it is your own choice.

I have had the distinct privilege of reading most, if not quite all of Rebecca's work in first or second draft form, and have grown to love how she delves into what it means to be feminine in a world of brutal violence, disdain, and ambivalence targeting women, mashing up our expectations of what will happen, because of course, we always know what will happen. In the many rooms of Rebecca Cuthbert's house, you will never receive quite what you expect.

This collection of stories goes a step further than much of her previous work, with these pieces often staged in the normal, the mundane, with settings that are, to each of us in this modern world, intimately familiar. With *The Hauntings Back Home*, even the carefully chosen title implies something wrong underneath the skin of our everyday being. A home is not simply a house, and a family not merely a collection of blood relatives.

The tales herein will grab you and gently hold you at the table until you finish your supper, and this is a meal that once tasted, you will want to revisit. From the shortest drabble to the longest near-novelette, Rebecca carves her way into your psyche with stories of families torn asunder, of lives rent in two or three or lost forever in some Elsewhere.

Let her guide you into her home and read you a story.

-Jonathan Gensler, July 2025

WHEN YOU WANDER IN THE WOODS

BY BEATRICE SHEEHAN

When you wander in the woods,

do not tell me that a branch snagged your hair

or that you tripped and ripped your jeans on a thorn bush;

thorns can't bite and branches can't tear.

When you wander in the woods,

do not tell me it was a shadow or the wind

or an overactive imagination;

you can't imagine hands grabbing for your legs.

When you wander in the woods,

do not tell me that the cuts on your stomach and cheeks

are just scratches from your untamed pet;

pets can't cut so deep that the flesh peeks out underneath.

When you wander in the woods,

do not tell me that you simply twisted your ankle

when you fell on the path;
the dirt can't twist bones or tear sinew.

When you wander in the woods,
do not tell me it was just an owl
hooting above in the trees;
owls can't wail and moan like tortured ghosts.

When you wander in the woods,
and a monster tries to snatch you away,
don't tell me it was the wind;
the wind cannot shake the ground so hard you fall down.

When you wander in the woods,
know that others have tried to make it through—
remember the others who are still stuck in those
cursed trees and sharp bushes and scratchy soil.

When you wander in the woods,
hear the wails of those forlorn souls
and heed the warnings I offer,
before you wander so long you are lost forever.

And when you wander in the woods,
if you make it back home,
do not tell me you were worried about me
and *that* is why you came back.

You were able to return because someone above took pity

on you and on me and on your poor oblivious parents, too;

and *they* let you pass through—that angel in those

devilish

woods.

DOWNSTAIRS AT THE SABINE

(THE NIGHT WATCHMAN OF A DECREPIT HOTEL DISCOVERS WHAT'S HIDING IN THE BOWELS OF THE GRAND BUILDING)

Marco had gotten the night watchman gig because his cousin's best friend knew the owner.

He needed the work, and the job sounded easy: Rounds every hour, basement to top floor. Take the stairs since the elevator's broken.

It was an old hotel, abandoned shortly after opening in the 50s. Empty ever since. The new owner had bought it at a tax auction and planned to turn it into luxury condos.

And though Marco didn't know anything about luxury, he could point a flashlight and climb stairs. If he ran into trouble, he could handle himself.

Not that he'd need to, he figured. The place was dead. A marble-tiled lobby, four floors with six suites each, and an empty swimming pool in the basement. Outside, a burned-out sign read *The Hotel Sabine.*

Marco walked the lobby, shining his flashlight over rusting luggage carts, broken-legged armchairs, and a sagging front desk. A small silver bell, covered in dust, still sat where the last person had rung it. And because he was bored, because it was his second night and the silence of that dim and cavernous place weighed on him more heavily than he thought it would, Marco stepped close to the desk and pressed a finger down on the bell's metal button.

Ding.

It rang true, chiming its proud little peal like no time had passed at all, like it was unbothered by the dankness and decay. The note echoed through the space behind and above Marco, traveling into the black corners and up to the lofted ceiling with its cobwebbed chandeliers.

But the sound intensified the quiet instead of breaking it, leaving it more oppressive than before. Marco had his earbuds in his pocket; he was tempted to plug them in and listen to some music or a podcast. But, he reasoned, what good was a watchman who couldn't hear an intruder? He took a sip of coffee from his thermos and headed to the grand staircase. Climbing up, his feet squelched on the water-stained stair runner that used to be red.

He'd reached the top and taken four steps down the left hallway when he heard a door bang shut downstairs.

His breath hitched in his chest and he stopped short, almost dropping his coffee. He debated his next move—run down the stairs yelling? Or turn off the flashlight for the element of surprise? Deciding on the second, he clicked off his light and set his thermos on the floor. He walked slowly, counting his steps, back to the stairs. Four. Then down, toes tentative on each step to avoid a fall. Twenty-six.

When his boots left the sodden carpet and met marble, he turned his flashlight on, aiming first at the large double doors that used to serve as the hotel's main entrance.

Boarded up, still, wood and nails covering cracked glass, just like they should.

Then to the right, at the door to the small office, behind the front desk. Closed. Marco walked quickly to it and tried the knob. Locked.

Same with a storage closet near the broken elevator.

Then there was the door Marco came in, hidden behind the fancy staircase. It led to a narrow hallway and out to the loading dock, behind the hotel. He and Sal were the only ones with keys, and Marco always locked it behind him. He checked it anyway. Still secure.

He played the beam over the corners of the lobby, underneath ratty console tables and behind chairs. That was just a bid for time, though—he knew he'd heard a door, not the scrape of furniture.

And there was only one door left.

The door to the basement.

As he walked toward it, hinges creaked and wood groaned and the door opened, letting out a warm puff of mildew-and-chlorine scented air.

Marco coughed and swore. His steel flashlight was all he had for a weapon. But whoever had run to the basement was trapped. The stairs were the only way out—even if the elevator worked, it stopped at the lobby. So once Marco got down there, it would just be him and a stranger, playing hide-and-seek.

He gripped the flashlight with his left hand and curled his right hand into a fist, drawing it back, ready to hit, and step by shaky step, he descended.

A bank of fluorescent lights to turn on would have been nice. But the building didn't have electricity. It had been cut off long ago, and wouldn't be reconnected until The Sabine was rewired with modern outlets and switches. And that, Sal had admitted, wasn't going to happen until he could find a few more investors.

Marco's flashlight was it.

He paused in the doorway, noting how warm it was in the basement. He shined his light across the pool deck and wiped sweat from his forehead, seeing nothing other than a pile of dry-rotted floatation devices, a fiberglass diving board, and a rickety lifeguard stand. Then he quickly stepped through the doorway and shined his light to the right and left, making sure no one was crouched there, waiting to attack him.

Across the empty pool, doors to the men's and women's changing rooms were closed. He walked to the edge of the pool, running his beam across the dry tiles in quick arcs. But there was no place for someone to hide in an empty swimming pool. No, Marco thought, the logical choice would be the locker rooms.

Marco didn't like the idea of being hemmed in with God-knew-who. He reminded himself it was probably just kids looking for kicks, or a homeless person wanting to get out of the weather. Not a violent criminal.

He circled the pool, careful that he didn't get too close to the edge. He wasn't far from the door to the women's changing room when something flew at him from the dark, knocking his flashlight from his hand. It made a dull ringing sound as it hit the tiles. Then he was being shoved, back back back, until his boot heels teetered over the void. His arms pinwheeled, but found no purchase, and he fell.

He heard a splash, felt water receive his body like a soft bed, and then his senses switched off and there was nothing.

Later, an eternity or a few minutes, he was being poked at. Prodded. Fingers on his neck, something heavy resting on his chest. A voice whispering *JesusChristJesusChristJesusChrist*. Marco opened his eyes.

Sal, the owner of the building, crouched over him. Marco saw relief wash across the other man's face.

"Thank God," said Sal. "I saw that you hadn't punched out on the app yet. I tried your cell and couldn't reach you, so I came looking. The fuck happened, man? And is that sweat or did you piss yourself?" Sal wiped his hand on the knee of his pants.

Marco sat up. They were in the empty swimming pool. The deep end. He felt his head, ran his hands over his face and chest. He was soaked. An uncomfortable bulge dug into his left thigh. He shifted; it was his crushed cell phone. "Shit," he said, looking at the phone in his hand, then, to Sal, "Am I hurt?"

Sal stood up and smoothed creases from his chinos. "How the hell should I know? Are you?" he said. "And what kind of dumbass falls into an empty pool? Tieg recommended you, said you were a good guy, but—"

"I didn't fall," interrupted Marco, trying to remember. "And I didn't piss myself. I was upstairs, and I heard a door…" He told Sal the story, right up to the shove—how he felt hands on his shoulders, empty space opening up behind him.

"Shit, man. Do you think they could still be here?" Sal took off his jacket and folded it over his arm. "I should call the police. And do you need to see a doctor?"

"No, no. No need for all that," Marco said, wanting to downplay how he'd let someone get past him his second night on the job. "I'm fine. And I probably just spooked some kid, maybe someone looking for a place to shoot up. What would the cops do, anyway?"

Sal didn't look convinced.

"Really. Let me take a look in the locker rooms, just in case. Then we'll get out of here," Marco said.

Sal shrugged. The two men walked to the shallow end and climbed up a short ladder. Marco's flashlight lay smashed on the pool deck.

The locker rooms were empty.

Marco went home.

That night, armed with a working flashlight, a cheap replacement phone, and an old hammer slung through his utility belt, Marco felt prepared. He'd popped two caffeine pills and arrived at The Sabine early, while it was still light out, so he could take a good look at all the doors and ground-floor windows. He collected his thermos from where he'd left it the night before and dumped cold coffee into the dry planter of what might have once been a large fern.

He knew he should check the basement, too. The locker rooms, all the toilet and shower stalls. But he couldn't make himself go down there again, or even stick his head through the doorway. Something about the dusky stairwell, the humid smell that came from below—it made Marco nauseous.

He wished that door had a lock.

Marco looked around the lobby for a solution. The meager light of the sun was fading already, and he needed to click on his flashlight. When its beam fell on a raggedy old sofa that slumped to the left, he smiled. Its upholstery was mouse-chewed and it smelled like urine, but it looked heavy, with a solid frame. He dragged it in front of the door to the basement and, grunting with the effort, stood it on its end, blocking the way. "No one out or in," he said out loud.

He smiled again, even chancing a whistle, but he stopped when the echo made it sound like someone was in the lobby with him, whistling too, in a kind of spooky duet.

He cleared his throat and climbed the stairs for another patrol.

Marco was on the third floor when he heard a crash from below, so loud that a tremor shook his boots.

This time, he didn't hesitate. He ran to the stairwell, taking the steps two at a time, panting as his lungs burned. He pulled the hammer from his belt as he reached the second floor and rounded the corner, his feet pounding mildewed carpet until he reached the top of the formal staircase.

"Who's there?" he demanded. "Show yourself!"

His flashlight beam skimmed the lobby's rotted furniture, the front desk, the boarded-up doors. Then it landed on the couch he'd used to block the basement stairwell. It was sitting right-side up several feet away from where he'd left it. Someone had moved it—pushed it over and out of the way. He walked slowly down the steps and toward the couch, keeping his light trained on it, ready for someone to jump out and yell "Boo!"

Instead, behind him, the bell on the front desk chimed.

Marco spun, renewed adrenaline washing up through his torso as the bell's echo faded. Sweat soaked the collar of his blue work shirt.

"Show yourself!" he yelled again, stepping sideways to keep the basement stairway in view. His chest felt tight, from both exertion and fear. "This is private property and you're trespassing!" He shined his light behind the front counter and across the closed office door.

Nothing.

Then footsteps, slapping down the basement stairs to the pool.

"Fucker!" Marco swore, angry that once again, he'd let someone get past him—someone skirting the walls, keeping to the shadows, toying with him.

Kids, he thought. Taking a cheap shot at him the night before, in the dark. He swore again and pulled the hammer from his belt.

Steeling himself, he marched to the doorway and stomped down the stairs. "You wanna play? I'll play!" he called. "Come on out and I'll teach you a new game."

No one answered. Marco held his breath and listened, ready to swing his hammer toward the next noise he heard.

But the next noise he heard didn't make sense.

A splash, then water lapping against something solid.

A woman's full-throated laughter.

Marco reached the bottom of the stairs and rushed through the doorway, bringing his flashlight up from hip level to sweep it across—

It went out.

Impossible. He'd just bought it. Loaded it with fresh batteries.

He heard more splashing, quieter this time, like strong arms cutting through calm water. He panicked, trying not to drop his hammer while he slapped at the flashlight, then shook it, *fuckfuckfuck* running through his head like an incantation.

It was no use. He shoved the dead flashlight into its loop on his belt, gripped the hammer harder, pulled out his new phone, and scrambled to light it up. But his fingers were sweating, wet, and the screen didn't respond. The best he could do was press the button for the home screen, getting a weak green glow. It was better than nothing. He held it out in front of him, trying not to notice how his hand trembled.

That's when he saw her.

A woman, almost, climbing out of the pool. She moved like liquid, her naked flesh all curves and no angles, wispy at the edges. Dark hair dripped over her shoulder and her eyes glowed a chemical blue.

She laughed again as he stared, but the sound didn't come from her. It came from the air around him and kept coming, swallowed and spit back by the gloom.

"What the—" Marco mumbled, trying to make sense of the woman, the water, the laughter.

She flicked her hair over her shoulder and arched her back, like she wanted to give him a better view.

He took a step toward her. Another.

Then the laughter died and she smiled at him, her lips stretching until her teeth showed, teeth too long, too sharp—

Marco screamed.

His feet moved by instinct, spinning him around and propelling him up the stairs. He exploded into the lobby, sprinted across it, and slammed into the service door under the stairs. The laughter came again, jabbing at him, ringing in his ears. He fumbled with the keys on his belt, fingers shaking, sweating more and more. Finally, he found the right key and jammed it into the lock.

He ran down the utility hallway, thankful that it was a straight shot. Another key to the loading dock, this one found faster, and he was out in the night air, gulping oxygen, hands on his knees, coughing.

Marco's brain, gone to jelly in the basement, solidified. Thoughts became clearer. He had saved Sal's number in his new phone that morning and scrolled to it now, finger tapping the name. But before it could ring he ended the call.

He'd let an intruder past him the night before. Then someone, something got the better of him again. And instead of investigating, he'd bolted like a frightened horse. If he called Sal to report this, he knew he'd be fired for sure.

Plus, he didn't think Sal would believe him. What he saw—it didn't make sense. Saw *and* heard, said a little voice inside him, but Marco ignored it. He was aware of the weird things sleep deprivation could do to a person—he'd worked enough third-shift jobs to experience them. And he hadn't eaten much that day, and with the caffeine pills...he wondered if it was a hallucination, part dream, his mind trying to sleep when his body wouldn't let it.

That or he did hit his head the night before, hard enough to knock something loose.

Anything but a woman-monster swimming in a pool that had been drained 70 years ago, he told himself.

Not that.

He sat on the loading dock until morning, then tapped the app on his phone screen that let him clock out.

He made sure the loading dock door had locked behind him, then went home to get some sleep.

Marco slept for 10 hours and skipped the caffeine pills.

He went to work.

This time, he brought two flashlights, both with fresh batteries. He had his hammer. He had his phone.

He told himself he wasn't avoiding the basement, just being thorough, when he started on the top floor, checking all six suites twice for locked doors, all hallway windows for tight latches. Then he moved to the fourth floor, checked six rooms. Then the third floor, six rooms. Second floor, six rooms.

Then he got to the lobby.

Before he stepped down onto the marble tiles, Marco pulled the second flashlight from his belt and clicked it on. Twice the brightness. But he wanted to have his hammer ready, too. He'd allow for his mind playing tricks on him the night before, but he knew he didn't push himself into the empty pool two nights ago. Someone, somehow, was getting in.

Or hadn't left.

That thought chilled him and he froze mid-step, left foot still on the stair behind him. He imagined someone watching him from behind moth-eaten curtains, skulking in murky corners.

Waiting for their opportunity to scare him, or worse. They could be watching him right now.

His mouth was dry but he forced himself to swallow.

Marco pushed one of the flashlights, still on, through a beltloop near his hip. It hung down at an angle and illuminated the floor to the right. It wasn't ideal, but it freed up a hand for his hammer.

He drew out his weapon and clutched it near the bottom of the shaft, so he could put some momentum into his swing. Should he need to swing.

And he waited. He waited for trouble, waited for tricks. Waited for a noise he shouldn't hear all alone in a ramshackle hotel.

An hour passed. He was supposed to do his rounds again, but that would mean turning away from the lobby, and Marco didn't want to do that—whoever was messing with him seemed to stick to the basement and first floor, so he would, too. He stood on the bottom step of the grand staircase, turning from right to left, like a lighthouse keeper scanning the sea.

He waited for that bell to ring or for furniture to move or for footsteps clomping away across the grimy floor.

But after two hours had passed, then three, his muscles cramping and his back aching, it wasn't chiming or scraping or stomping that made Marco stop his steady turning.

It was a cry for help.

And it came from downstairs. From the basement.

Fuck, Marco thought.

He hesitated.

"Help!" The cry came again. A woman's voice.

"Who's there?" Marco yelled, leaving his post and stepping closer to the open basement door, around the heavy couch, shining his light in and down.

"Help!" was the response. "Help!" again, desperate. *"Please!"* Splashing. Frantic.

Marco groaned, but moved. He tucked his hammer under his arm to reach for his phone, pressing the home screen button and activating voice-to-text as he ran, telling Sal to call the police—someone was in trouble, someone in the basement. He hoped the message wouldn't be garbled, that the thick basement walls wouldn't keep the text from sending in the first place.

Marco hit the last step and didn't slow down; he ran through the doorway, one flashlight scanning the room, the other bobbing crazily at his hip.

He saw her.

There, in the water.

He froze. His hammer slipped from beneath his arm, the dull clink of metal on tile reverberating in the hollow space. His cell phone followed, clattering near his feet.

Marco gaped as her dark head surfaced, went down again, surfaced. "Help!" she called, sputtering the word, mouth taking in water. Her arms splashed wildly and Marco caught sight of one perfect breast as it broke from the water only to sink beneath it again.

He squeezed his eyes shut and gave his head a hard shake. He opened his eyes, and the scene was the same. He was awake, he was sure of it, and he was watching a woman drown. Watching, and not helping.

The woman's arms went straight up, pale hands above the surface before she disappeared.

Marco dropped the flashlight he'd been holding and dove into the water, kicking toward the spot where he'd last seen her.

The flashlight shoved into his beltloop winked in and out. It wasn't waterproof. In its faulty beam he saw an arm, floating, stretching, dark hair waving like a flag in the wind. She faced away from him, tipping forward, shifting and rolling in the water. He didn't see any bubbles coming from her nose or mouth.

The light failed as Marco got close, but he could reach her now. He grabbed her arm, pulled her toward him and around, pressed her chest tight to his so he could make for the surface. His panicked mind tried to recall the moves for CPR, how many times he was supposed to pump her chest, whether he should breathe into her mouth.

The flashlight came on again just as it pulled free from his beltloop, somersaulting slowly toward the bottom of the pool. In its fitful light, Marco saw the woman's eyes open, a blue brighter than the pool tiles. Her hands found his shoulders and squeezed; they were almost to the surface, and Marco thought *thank God she's alive* until the hands squeezed harder, nails like claws tearing through his thick work shirt, into his flesh, bloodying the water around them. In the flashlight's final spin he saw the woman's mouth open, saw her teeth, white and sharp, coming for him, for his neck, and their heads emerged from the water just in time for

Marco to scream, to hear himself screaming, to hear his anguish echo off the concrete walls, to hear the woman's laugh ring out, the same laugh from the night before, a laugh so full of joy it shook both of their bodies, even in the water, bobbing as they were. Marco's pants and shirt and work boots had become so heavy, so waterlogged, that when the woman let go of his ribboned shoulders it was he who sank, down and then lower, until his boots hit the bottom of the pool and the beautiful woman with the sharp nails and sharp teeth was only a memory from a life that wasn't his anymore.

At the bottom of the deep end of the empty pool in the basement of The Sabine, Sal and two uniformed officers stood over Marco's body.

Sal tried not to shudder in front of the other men, but he didn't like how Marco's open eyes stared past them to the high raftered ceiling. "Who would do this?" he asked.

"Animals, maybe," said one of the officers. "Rats?"

"But wouldn't rats have...um...*eaten* more?" Sal asked. He let out a queasy burp.

Both officers shrugged.

Sal tried not to vomit, looking at the inside of Marco's throat, the pipes and strings and toggles that no one was ever meant to see. The warmth of the basement wasn't helping; flies had already found the wounds in Marco's flesh. Then there was the smell. A flush of dizziness hit Sal; he toppled but caught himself with a hand on Marco's dead thigh.

He yelled and threw himself backward, scrabbling away like a crab.

He wiped his hand on his pants. "Why is he so wet?" he asked.

But the officers, again, just shrugged and said there'd be an investigation, that Sal should hand over his phone for that last garbled message, give them the keys to the hotel. They thanked him for cooperating, and asked him to make a statement at the station, which Sal said of course he'd do—right away.

He walked to the shallow end of the pool and climbed the short ladder to the deck. He headed for the stairwell, then paused and turned back. "Marco was a good guy," he called to the officers. "He was a good guy, and I was gonna tell him—" Sal stopped and shook his head. What did it matter? He walked through the doorway and up the stairs, picking up speed as he crossed the filthy lobby, jogging down the utility hallway.

He made it outside just in time to throw up over the guardrail of the loading dock.

Sal hadn't gotten the chance to tell Marco that he was letting him go—that it was all falling apart, that he hadn't been able to get those investors after all. That The Sabine wouldn't be refurbished as luxury condos anytime soon. That for now and the foreseeable future, the hotel would stay just as it was and had been, holding its silence close, keeping all its secrets.

THE ONE THAT GOT AWAY

The summers are for tourists here—dumbass shoreline boat cruises and overpriced ice cream, Black Spruce Bay shot glass souvenirs, $4.99 each. But winters—ice fishing, hard drinking, swapping stories at the tavern while numb toes thaw—those are for the locals.

Except this year, for the first time in three decades, the river that dumps into the bay hasn't frozen, and there's no creeping crust of blackish ice on our rocky shores.

Just dark, still water, and a wind that cuts sharp as a steel blade.

"Feels weird, no ice fishing this year," says Wayne. "Ah, well. One more, Jessie-Girl."

Wayne is a regular at the Dogfish Tavern. I've worked here 10 years, since I started bussing tables at 16. Wayne's been here that long, too.

"You've *one-mored* that rye bottle down to a mouthful," says Lynn, the owner. She mostly helps with the register and, when we're busy, heads back to the kitchen to deep-fry the only four menu items we serve. "And I only opened it two days ago."

Lynn's in her 60s and works seven nights a week, even with her left arm missing below the elbow. "Fishing accident," she told me when she hired me. She left it at that so I did, too. She's kind of a bitch, but I try not to hold that against her. Get stuck here long enough and it's inevitable.

"You sound like my ex-wife," Wayne says, which is what he says every time Lynn or me or anyone tells him to slow down. But he does seem to be swigging it faster than usual this week.

"I'll take that as a compliment," says Lynn. "She was smart enough to leave your ass." Then she cackles.

Wayne laughs too, then he gets serious again. "It's this damn weather," he says. "It's just not right. Cold enough to freeze, but the ice in the fjord wouldn't fill this rye glass." He shakes his head, and I'm surprised to see that Lynn looks upset, too.

"Yeah, turns out global warming's real after all, huh?" I say, but neither answers, so I grab a tray and a bleach rag to go bus dirty tables.

The first week of February, a kid goes missing.

His name's Grey Larson and he just turned 15. He and his friend were playing lacrosse by the fjord's edge, and the ball went into the water. Grey said he'd get it. His friend looked down to tighten a string on his stick. He heard a shout and a splash, and Grey was gone.

They spend time looking for him, of course. Boats go out. Divers in thermal wetsuits.

All they find is his broken lacrosse stick, marks on the handle like sharp teeth got a hold of it.

A couple days later I get to work and find Lynn staring out the tavern's window, looking at the spot where the river pours into the bay.

"No ice," she mutters, but not to me. "We need ice."

"We need a fuck of a lot more than *that*."

My voice comes out harsher than I mean it to—the whole town's in mourning and Lynn's worried about ice?

But she doesn't react to my words or my mood. I leave her alone and head to the kitchen to clock in.

The second person to not make it home is Jake LeRoy, a trapper who brags about doing things "the old-fashioned way," just like his ancestors. He's been ticketed by the Mounties for poaching a few times.

No one likes him, but still.

It takes two days for his severed leg to wash up onshore: flesh ragged, bone splintered.

They ID it by his bright orange bootlaces.

"Dead then, for sure," says Wayne. He's at the bar with all three of my brothers, plus a few other locals. "Can't survive that kinda blood loss, eh?"

My brother Chuck shakes his head. The others just look into their drinks like they're reading tea leaves.

Lynn's been quiet all night, taking lots of smoke breaks. Leaving me to do all the work.

"What the fuck could *do* that to a man?" asks my brother Billy. "We don't have anything that big in the bay."

Lynn hurries away like she smells something burning. I see Wayne follow her with his eyes. If I didn't know better I'd think they were sleeping together.

"Coulda been a bear," says Chuck. "They'll tear you up good."

"Sure," says my youngest brother, Johnny. "But where's the blood? It's not there. I looked."

"You looked?" says Chuck. "Alone? You crazy? Whatever did that's still—"

"Out there. I know." Johnny drains his glass, plunks it on the counter, and slams down a few toonies. "Keep the change, Sis," he tells me, and puts on his coat to leave.

"Take it easy, Jackrabbit Johannsen," calls Billy after him. "No more tracking tonight! Go straight home."

No one laughs at the joke.

"And stay away from the bay, eh?" Wayne yells.

Johnny just raises a hand.

The gesture could mean anything.

When Johnny goes missing a few days later, I replay that night in my mind, over and over. I know Chuck and Billy do, too.

None of us eat or sleep. They skip shifts at the cannery and look for Johnny every day, but they won't let me come. "Too cold, too dangerous," they say, but I can't stay home alone—our parents have been dead for years and with Johnny gone, too, the house feels like a mausoleum.

There's no place for me to go but the goddamn Dogfish.

Lynn comes behind the bar and watches me cut lemons. The slices are crooked and uneven and I don't give a shit. I dump them into their cup in the fruit tray, then dig the jar of maraschino cherries out of the bar fridge and refill that cup, too. The lime slices are skunky, but we don't have any fresh ones so I leave them.

"Jess," she says after a few minutes. "Try to be a little more careful with the cash drawer tonight, eh? Or maybe just leave the money stuff to me. Totals have been off three nights running."

I'm filling the bar sinks though there's barely anything to wash. But I can't do nothing. I don't look up.

"Yeah. Sure."

"And," she adds, "not to be harsh, but you forgot to clear the high-tops last night. I had to do it myself this morning."

I shut off the tap. Anger pools and rises like floodwater in my chest.

"Sorry if I've been a little *distracted*, Lynn. Don't know if you've heard? My *brother* is missing."

Her mouth settles into a straight line and her eyes glint.

"Of course. Of *course* I know," she says. "And I've been going easy on you because of it. Half the time you're spaced out, forgetting to do things or doing them twice, but do *I* throw temper tantrums? No. I don't. And you know what else? You're not the only one around here with *worries*."

I can't believe she's doing this. Calling my grief a temper tantrum. Acting like business at her stupid fucking bar is more important than Johnny.

"Ohhh. That's right!" I say, smacking my palm into my forehead like I can't believe my stupidity. "The bay! People disappearing left and right but you're mad about the *bay* not freezing. Sorry there's no ice fishing, Lynn! Sorry your bar profits are down! That's *way* worse than my brother probably being dead."

I know I've gone too far; I wait for her to tell me I'm fired. Instead, she backs down.

"Jessie," she says, "calm down, honey. I'm sorry."

She never calls me *honey* and from her it sounds grotesque. She's acting weird, too. Her eyes are wide; they dart down and back up. She takes a slow step away from me, then another.

I'm squeezing something in my left hand, tight enough that my fingers ache. I look; it's the fruit knife, sharp blade pointing out.

At her.

She backs up again but hits the counter.

"Just forget it," I say, and throw the knife into the sudsy water. I don't forgive her but I want her to go away.

She stays, though, frozen in my peripheral vision like prey until I turn my back on her to dust liquor bottles.

We don't speak for the rest of the night.

I can't shut my brain off.

Without knowing what happened to Johnny, all I can do is speculate. Each scenario I imagine is worse than the one before. I wonder what his last thoughts were. If he screamed or didn't get the chance to. If he went quickly or suffered.

Same as Grey, there's no body.

Same as Jake, there's no blood.

The Mounties don't advertise it, but they don't know shit.

No one does.

I go to work and come home, make tea that goes cold. I lose track of the days. Nod or shrug when spoken to, at least most of the time.

But if one more half-drunk townie tells me they're sorry about Johnny I'll stab them in the throat with my pen.

When Chuck and Billy find Johnny's toque snagged on a rock at the bay's mouth, it doesn't make anything better.

Later that evening, I catch the end of a conversation between Wayne and Lynn, who's still keeping her distance from me. I pretend to clean a high top behind them so I can eavesdrop better.

"...don't start on all that again," he's telling her. "It won't help."

"Fine," she snaps. "No one would listen before. Why would they now?"

"They listened. But listening and believing are two different things, Lynnie."

He sounds tired.

"It'd stop if the bay would just *freeze*," she says. "All these years, we haven't had any trouble. All these years." Then she starts in on the rye, too—no mixer, no chaser. Just throws it back and swallows. "And now it's back like a goddamned ghost."

And that's when I know it's about more than missing ice and slow business.

Lynn is keeping something from me.

She catches me crying in the kitchen.

"Try not to think about it, Jess," she says, and after hesitating, pats my shoulder.

I jerk back, flinging her hand away, and her look of surprise only pisses me off more.

"Don't think about it," I say. Heat floods my face and I wipe at my eyes. "Don't think about how my brother's *gone*? Don't think about whatever the fuck is picking us off one by one?"

"Fine," she says. "I was only trying to—"

"Who's gonna be next?" I ask her. My voice sounds like someone else's—too loose, too shrill. The next words fall out unplanned: "Maybe it'll be *you*."

She looks at me like I've slapped her, and for a moment, I wonder what it would feel like if I did: if the crack of my palm against her face would be worth the sting. Worth the consequences.

Maybe.

But I push past her, escaping to the blur of working the bar, where I pour and shake and nod and smile and put off the long sleepless night waiting for me at home, at least for a few more hours.

In the dead of winter, when the only reliable way to get around is by snowmobile, only about 400 people live here in Black Spruce Bay.

With three of our own gone, the locals lose faith in the Mounties, ignore the warnings, and head out in twos and threes to motor around the bay and comb the woods. Rumours whizz through the tavern like darts, and I pay attention to every word.

"Craig Thorne saw grizzly tracks."

"Emmett Brown heard something growling in the woods."

"It's a Loup-garou and you fuckin' know it."

It's late, and soon only Wayne and my brothers are left at the bar.

"Tell you what," says Chuck to no one in particular. "If I can't get Johnny back, I'm sure as shit getting revenge."

Billy nods, but Lynn, more than half-cut, says "Leave it, boys. There's things in tha' water you don't wanna mess with. 'Specially at night."

Then she turns and heads to the kitchen; before I follow her I hear Chuck say to Billy, "Come on. We're going home to get the damn canoe."

She's not in the kitchen but I find her out back, smoking by the dumpster.

I'm sick of the sulky silences—mine and hers—so I get right to it.

"What aren't you saying?" I ask her.

She shakes her head like it's not important.

I want to backhand her. Tell her to cut her shit. But I think I should try nice first, so I ball my hands into fists and stick them in my apron. I barely feel the cold.

"My brother is missing," I say, slowly, like I'm breaking the news to a child. "My baby brother. If you know anything—"

"I don't!" Lynn says. But she answered too fast and she won't look at me. I give up on nice quick.

"Liar. I *heard* you talking to Wayne."

She closes her eyes, inhales and blows out like she's trying not to puke. I smell the booze on her breath. "Tha' was a long time ago, Jess."

"What was?"

"Tha' night—" she says, and stops—opens her eyes. Throws down her spent cigarette and starts over. She tries to annunciate but still misses some consonants. I haven't seen her this wasted in a long time. Maybe not ever. "Th'night I lost Harold. Th'night something...*took* him from me."

Harold was Lynn's husband. She's been widowed for as long as I've known her. She doesn't talk about him, at least not to me.

"What happened?" I ask, voice flat. I can't make myself feel sympathy for her. My own loss is too big and it takes up all the room inside me.

"I'm not proud abou' it," she says and sniffs. "Bu' we were desperate. Th'bay hadn't frozen, so we took a'vantage. Waited until late t'go..."

"Jesus Christ! Sober up. To *what*?"

She jumps a little, then focuses, as well as she can, on my face.

"Fine. Go *poachin'*, okay, Jessie? We were poachin'."

I wait while she lights another cigarette. It hangs from her lips as she pockets her lighter, then scoops a handful of snow from the lid of the dumpster and squeezes it into a dense clump. She holds it to her forehead like an ice pack.

It seems to help. When she speaks again she sounds almost like herself.

"Harold's fishing license ha' lapsed. I din't have the tavern then. Got it with the insurance money, after. Tha's part of why... Anyway. He hooked something big—I 'member him laughing. He'd barely started pullin' when he wen' overboard—there was a scream an' a splash."

"A shark?"

She drops her melting snowball. It leaves behind a red mark, like a brand, on her forehead.

"You know as well as I do tha' there's no sharks in th'bay! Jus' *listen* to me! When Harold wen' in I panicked. I grabbed the flashlight bu' my hands were wet and I los' my grip; it rolled on the deck, jus' a thin beam bobbin' across the water. I wen' after him myself—climbed over and reached for him and grabbed his han' and then—" She takes a deep drag, blows out smoke, forces her lips to shape the words, and they're slow now, exaggerated, but clear: "I saw its *head*. Black and sleek with eyes like pits. Scaly snout. Sharp teeth. It had him. He screamed again, and I pulled, and then his hand came away... Only his *hand*, Jessie. The rest of him was just *gone*. And before I could even take a breath it had me too—like it wanted Harold's hand and since mine was attached it'd swallow them both."

She's crying now, deep in the memory of her long-ago tragedy.

Fuck Harold and fuck you, I think. But I'm listening.

"The boat ran into the rocks," she continues. She wipes snot and tears on her sleeve. "They found me nearby the next morning. Unconscious, hypothermic. I spent two weeks in the hospital."

I think I understand now—about the ice, about the bay.

"Are you saying it's the same thing? What took Johnny? This...animal, that it came back?"

"Not animal," she whispers. "Monster. Yes."

"Monster? That's crazy."

"That's what they said! But it happened! I *know* it did. Oh, Harold..."

I almost say there are no monsters, but what do I know? She's right about the sharks—we've never seen one in our bay. And if a grizzly or even a pack of wolves had taken Johnny and the others, there would have been blood on the snow. The only real possibility is that they went into the water, but they wouldn't have done that on their own.

Something must have taken them. Pulled them in.

"Fine," I say. "But if you're so sure why didn't you tell anyone? Not when Grey went missing. Not when Jake went missing. You just kept your mouth shut and *let* it take my brother?"

I'm repulsed by her. She sees it on my face and tries to grab my hand, but I step back. The tip of her cigarette grazes my wrist, but the pain feels separate from me.

"You believe me? *They* didn't. Not then. They wouldn't now."

"Who didn't?"

"Everyone! The locals, the Mounties. They called me crazy, too! Said I made it up!"

"You could have tried."

"I *did!* Back then. And God, did it cost me."

She throws down her cigarette. It hisses in the snow.

"They wouldn't even hear you out? Your *arm* was gone."

But I can picture it: a woman distraught, hypothermic, out of her mind, trying to tell men that she'd seen a monster. Of course they didn't believe her.

"I was on the rocks; they said it could have been a grizzly... And Harold was missing," she says. "Jessie, they *investigated* me. Said they had to—that it was all *standard procedure*. I heard the whispers—*murderer, gold-digger, black widow*. After a time it died down, but when I bought this place, they looked into me *again*. More suspicion. More rumours. Like I'd feed my husband to a monster for insurance money! You can't blame me for keeping quiet this time, Jessie. You can't."

I stare. The brand on her forehead is fading. Just a faint pink blotch.

"Yes, I can," I say. "And I do. Blame you."

I tell myself to walk away. To go inside, clock out, go home, lock myself in my bedroom and scream and scream and scream. I turn to do just that when I feel her clutch at my arm, fingers digging in.

"If even part of the bay would've frozen, Jess—"

I spin on my heel and my fist smashes into her face.

She covers her bleeding nose and I look at my aching hand—I didn't mean to, but she's still talking, blubbering: "—he wouldn't have been taken!"

"No!" I spit. "No. He was taken because *you* didn't speak up!"

I'm shaking, but I don't know if it's from cold or anger. Then I think of my brothers—*We're going home to get the damn canoe*—and my stomach drops.

"Oh, God. Whatever it is, it'll get Billy and Chuck next, because they're going out there, after it, and my family, my entire fucking *family*, you cowardly bitch, will be *gone*."

"I'm sorry, Jess." She comes toward me again. "I'm just so sorry..."

I grab her shoulders to push her away but then the idea hits me—crazy, maybe, like I called Lynn, like others called her—but that's exactly how I feel: reckless, unhinged. And I would do anything to save my brothers. Try anything. A long shot's worth a shot.

Still, I won't be able to go through with it if she's awake.

I pull her closer like I'm going to hug her, then grab her hair and slam her head against the side of the building.

The sound makes vomit rise in my throat but I swallow it down. This might be the only way. Even a small chance of saving my brothers is one I have to take.

What kind of sister would I be if I didn't?

Lynn's out cold, and lighter than I thought she'd be. When I drag her around the side of the building to her snowmobile, I see that Wayne's sled is gone. Good. I'd hate to have to hurt him, too. I flop her limp body on the back like a sack of flour and fish in her pocket for the key. To keep her from flying off, I sit on one of her legs.

Then I leave the lights off and drive, fast as I can, down to the bay.

She comes to as I'm tugging her toward the water's edge.

"Jessie?" she mumbles. "Jessie what're y'doing?"

I realize I'm crying. Stupidly, stupidly crying. I struggle to hold onto my anger, to remember why I'm doing this. I remind myself that Lynn is awful. That Johnny would still be alive if it wasn't for her—that she let people die because she was afraid she'd be called names.

"Shut up!" I sob. "If I give it what it wants, maybe it'll leave." My legs threaten to give out; darkness blurs the edges of my vision, but I have to keep going. "Maybe it'll still remember you. Maybe it still *wants* you."

I pick up a rock the size of my fist. It's hard to make my fingers close around it; my arm feels weak and rubbery.

"*What?* No—"

"The one that got away."

"Jess, please, no, please—"

But it's too late to stop now. I've gone this far and I have to protect my brothers. It doesn't matter what happens to me after.

I lift it high and smash the rock down on her forehead.

She goes quiet. I throw my weapon and hear the splash. Then, just like I hoped, a scaled back breaks the surface; it shimmers in the weak moonlight, moving with the bonelessness of a snake.

"Jessie!" I hear behind me.

I startle. It's Chuck's voice.

"What are you *doing*?"

I look behind me. Billy's dragging the canoe. He drops it. My brothers run toward me. My last two brothers. My only brothers.

I thought I'd have this done by the time they got here.

"*Jessie!* Jess, *stop!*"

But it doesn't matter.

"Jessica, *please!*"

In that moment, I can see on their faces how much they love me. That they would do anything for me.

But I feel the same way and I'm not the fragile thing they think I am.

So I take another heavy, wet step and shove Lynn into the water, sending her toward her destiny.

A sleek, dark head rises from the bay.

My brothers reach me, pull me back from the shoreline. I don't fight them.

They hold me tight as we watch, together, what could end it all.

GHOST IN THE GAS STATION BATHROOM

I hate cleaning the men's room at the gas station where I work.

He's there every time I open the door with my mop and bucket of bleach water. Middle aged with pitted cheeks and the look of a cornered animal—eyes wild and rolling. He's scrubbing his hands at the sink: frantic, blood everywhere. It's spattered in suds on the mirror and soaks his sleeves to the elbow. It covers his shirt—I can see it in the reflection.

And then, each time, he turns around—toward the door, and I don't think it's me he's seeing—his eyes go wide and he opens his mouth in a scream I can't hear. His body spasms; holes open in his chest. One in his forehead. And he goes down. Half a second later, and the bathroom is empty again. Just the usual piss on the walls and garbage on the floor.

The first time I saw him I had a panic attack and had to go home. I'd just started as third-shift cashier, needing extra money after my divorce. The second time I saw him I only sobbed, but my boss didn't believe me and accused me of seeing a spider instead.

I don't talk about it anymore, and I guess seeing him regularly has made him a little less scary—and being less scared, I got curious. Now, I kill the empty hours at work by thinking of what might've happened to him. I made a list on the back of a receipt:

1. He killed someone in a fit of passion—a married lover whose husband hunted him down, chasing him here and kicking in the bathroom door before hitting him with five bullets.

2. He killed someone in a robbery gone wrong—no one was supposed to be home. He tripped an alarm, ran, and was found at this gas station after a BOLO went out. The cops used a battering ram on the door and put five bullets in him.

3. He was innocent. The blood all over him is from someone he tried to *save*, maybe a stranger, maybe someone he loved. And police chased him, so he ran. They found him here and shot him five times before he could say a word in his own defense.

I've tried to talk to him once or twice. Dumb stuff, like "Hello" and "What's your name" and "I'm Tina, I work here." He's never responded. I don't know if that's a choice or a condition of his penance. To go through it, again and again—*scrub scrub scrub, bang bang bang bang bang*—without being able to talk about it.

What's really fucked up about it all, though, is that I've gotten kind of attached. I still hate opening that door each night, but now, after what—five months?—if he weren't there, I think I'd be disappointed. Lonely? Because the other guy who works the shift with me—Donny—wears headphones the whole time, restocking shelves to what sounds like 80s hairband ballads.

So, in a way, it's just me and the ghost, whoever he is. *Was.* Whatever he did. And I know I could play Nancy Drew—investigate clues, track down witnesses—but I won't. The truth is always less interesting, and every solved mystery becomes just another sad story. And the world is already too full of those.

Tonight it's slow. Tuesdays always are. Not many folks out needing gas or lotto tickets or beef jerky or whatever. A couple folks in to buy six-packs. One lady needing three bags of chips. Donny left early, claimed he had a headache. I didn't care. He's not really here when he's here anyway.

But at about 2 a.m., the bell above the door rings and I look up from the doodle I'm making, and it's *him.* The guy. The ghost.

My mouth drops open. I freeze. Then I see his eyes, wide and glassy, and the knife clutched in his hand. I think, *That's a huge knife. What does he need a knife like that for?*

And I'm still wondering when he's around the counter, in my face, towering over me, and it seems like no time has passed, like he was in the doorway and I blinked and now he's not, now he's *on* me—that big knife against my throat, the other hand gripping my shoulder so hard I know it's already bruising. He's spitting at me, talking, but through his teeth, and God he smells. Body odor but something chemical, too. And burnt hair. Sweat runs down his neck into his collar. He's furious. I haven't done anything to him, but he's furious.

I manage to hit the silent alarm under the counter, and I want to put my hands up, like people do in the movies, but I can't raise my arms; my muscles have turned to water. He's blocking all the light and taking all the air. I can't breathe. He whisper-yells at me to open the cash drawer, and I do, shaking so hard it takes me three tries to hit the right buttons. He grabs the money, not that there's much, and shoves it down the front of his pants. He won't take the knife away. I think he'll go but he doesn't. He's swearing at me, "Where's-the-safe-open-the-fucking-safe-you-fucking-bitch-fuck-open-it-stupid-whore-fuck-fuck," on and on, and I know he's high as a kite, not in his right mind, but I try explaining there is no safe. We don't have a safe; we do two cash drops a day at the bank. The manager does. I tell him all this, tripping over the words and saying it again, but he isn't listening, and he grips my shoulder tighter and I cry out from the pain and he shoves me against the rack of cigarettes and they fall around our feet with soft little plops.

I don't know how I get from there, standing, to the floor, lying on my side several feet away. I cough. I cough and spit; I'm bleeding. It's coming from my mouth. I spit it on the floor. I try to feel my stomach. My hand won't move. It's underneath me. Pinned. I can move my eyes but not my neck. The man's boots step over me. The knife clatters to the tiles near my head. I'm cold. I need to turn off the air conditioning. But it's March. There is no air conditioning. It's March. I'm so cold.

A cop comes through the door, gun drawn. There's another behind him, yelling into his radio. They run past me. I can't roll over to watch, but I know they'll find the man in the bathroom. I know he's trying to wash his hands, and I know they'll never come clean. Too much blood. All of it mine.

I know what happens next, too. I've seen it so many times.

There. The shouting. The gunshots. I count them: *One. Two. Three. Four. Five.* In the bathroom, the man is falling.

I close my eyes.

And there it is. Mystery solved, and I was right. Just another sad story, not so interesting after all.

THE VINES THAT BIND

(A WOMAN TAKES ON HER DEAD
MOTHER-IN-LAW—AND LOSES)

We buried my mother-in-law, Bobbi, midway through October.

She'd always loved the fall—she canned applesauce, made pies, exclaimed over every half-dead fucking leaf.

So when my sons, Henry and Noah, wanted to decorate her new grave with mums and gourds, my husband said yes. And because he said yes, I spent $53 at the farmers' market and a Saturday afternoon "making Nanny's grave pretty."

I didn't mind much, then. I thought it was the last trouble I'd have to go to for that miserable hag.

I was wrong.

Almost seven blissful months passed without her.

No calls in the middle of the night because she "heard a noise" outside. No passive-aggressive comments about how "modern" I was for having short hair. No torturous Sunday dinners that she insisted on having at 4 o'clock in the afternoon despite the fact that lunch had only been three hours before and no one was hungry.

Then, for Mother's Day, because it would have been weird if I said I didn't want to, we bought a bunch of daisies and carnations and drove to the cemetery. Henry and Noah fought over who would lay the flowers at the headstone until Troy divided the bouquet in half, saying "Simple problem, simple answer."

Just like my husband to solve one tiny parenting problem and gloat like he lifted more than a single damn finger at home.

We parked, walked to Bobbi's grave at the edge of the church property, and saw that it was overrun by new green vines, their leaves like arrows pointing in every direction.

"Well I'll be!" Troy said. "Pumpkin vines!"

"Pumpkins?"

To me they looked like weeds.

"Or gourds. Must have rotted down and seeded themselves."

He smiled and teared up like an idiot, as if his sainted mother had somehow manifested a miracle.

"We should pull them out," I said, and leaned over to grab hold of one.

Troy stopped me.

"No way!" he said. "Let's see what they grow. It'll be fun."

The boys were listening. They jumped up and down. I smiled tightly.

"Honey," I said. "There are rules to the upkeep here." I pointed at the sign we'd passed, over by the gate. "Plots have to be kept tidy. No plant growth beyond the sides of the headstones." I looked at the boys and pulled a face. "Too bad. But rules are rules!" I leaned down again and wrapped my hand around a vine to pull.

The goddamn thing was covered in little spikes. I jerked my hand back: tiny translucent spines covered my palm.

"Babe," said Troy, and he only called me that when he wanted to win an argument, "I know Old Burt, the caretaker here. Mom played bridge with his wife Lollie, remember? Over at the edge here, I'm sure he wouldn't mind if we bent the rules a little. Especially for Mom."

I smiled and it stretched my face tight as plastic wrap on leftovers.

"Well," I said. "If it's for *Mom*."

He didn't hear the edge to my voice. He just smiled and ushered the boys toward the car.

Burt did indeed bend the rules for Bobbi, thanks in large part to the generous steakhouse gift card Troy greased his palm with, and by June, the vines grew gooseneck gourds the size of my foot. The boys picked them and pretended they were guns, shooting each other and diving behind headstones. Troy ignored them and prayed over his mom's grave while I stood beside him, head bowed, thinking of what to get my coworker for her baby shower.

The sound of crying made me look up.

Noah walked toward us, his hands full of pulpy, broken gourd.

Troy took the pieces from him, ready to scold, but stopped short. His face had that look again—like he was witnessing the birth of Jesus.

"Hon?" he said, his voice shaking.

He held up something metallic.

"How... How did your brooch get *inside* this? Oh, Mom..."

Ice crept up my back.

That brooch—tarnished metal and fake rubies.

His mother had given it to me the year before: costume jewelry from her own collection, cheap and tacky. Not that I hated *all* her stuff—she had a pair of freshwater pearl earrings the size of gumdrops that I loved, and I *told* her so, more than once—but a codicil in her will stipulated she'd be buried in those.

That brooch, though—that wouldn't even dress up a dog turd.

I'd dropped it into Bobbi's casket before they'd closed the lid the day of her funeral, whispering that she could have it back.

But there in the cemetery, with the boys watching, I changed the look on my face from disgust to happy wonderment.

"How funny!" I said. "It must have fallen off the day of the funeral..."

"And the gourd grew around it!" Troy finished. He winked at the boys. "Or maybe Nanny put it there."

I wasn't a gardener, but I didn't think gourds could do that. A sense of unease settled into my stomach and lodged there like a hairball.

Troy was grinning, though—of course he was—showing it to Noah. Noah stopped sniffling. His brother walked closer so he could see, too.

"You lost it and Nanny found it for you!" Henry said.

Troy wiped at his eyes.

I didn't want to touch it, but I took the brooch from him and put it in my pocket.

July was busy. August a scramble. We didn't get back to the cemetery until September.

By then, the vines had stretched around the headstone and behind it, into the brush that bordered the property, like they sought out wildness.

Troy and the boys trooped into the tall grass. I stayed on the lawn, but I could see them: long green arms reaching around scrub brush and saplings, creeping to the right and left, claiming whatever they could reach with their thin looping fingers. Spiny stems. Glossy leaves, some spotted with white, others eaten through by insects. Gourds and squash in orange and yellow and green and pink.

"*What the fuck?*" I murmured before I could stop myself.

There were just so many.

"Hon, your *language*." Troy scowled but I ignored him.

"We have to get rid of these," I said. "If they plant themselves again they'll take over the whole graveyard by next year."

"Of course you'd want to kill them," Troy said, heedless now of the boys himself. "Why would you like anything my mother did?

Why would you want to *nurture* something that gives her so much *joy?*"

"*Gives?*" I said. "Can you hear yourself? *Gives?* Present tense? Your mother is *dead*, Troy. Dead. Gone. Yet you *still* seem more worried about her than about me."

Troy's mouth twisted. He looked at the boys, then at me.

"That's what this is?" Troy said. "Jealousy? Mom told me she thought you were, but I said no, couldn't be—"

"*What?*"

I put my hands in the pockets of my sweatshirt, balling my fists, reminding myself the boys were there. But if Troy didn't get away from me, right then, I'd slap him.

"Take the boys to the car."

He grabbed their hands, but before he stalked off, he spat "You're *not* killing Mom's pumpkins."

"Yeah!" said Henry, joining in to take his dad's, and grandmother's, side. Typical. "Don't kill Nanny's pumpkins!"

"Yeah!" echoed Noah. He copied everything his brother did.

I clenched my jaw and watched them go. When they were out of sight, I looked down. The base of one of the vines rested near my sandaled foot.

I kicked at it.

Stupid goddamn vines.

Stupid goddamn gourds.

Stupid husband, stupid marriage, stupid fucking mother-in-law still causing fights even after she'd kicked it.

"*Bitch*," I said out loud.

A squat heirloom pumpkin sat a foot away, its blank face staring at me.

"*Bitch!*"

I brought my heel down on it, smashing it flat and bruising the arch of my foot.

"Fuck!" I said, hopping. "Fuck fuck fuck!"

Troy was right. My language sucked. And I hated fighting in front of the boys. I tried not to cry, counting backward from 10.

When the flush of pain passed, I kicked at the mess. I thought I'd see a hidden stone or stick—my foot throbbed.

Instead, I found the lower portion of Bobbi's dentures, chipped and cracked in places.

Chipped and cracked because she'd been wearing them the day she fell down the basement steps.

It happened on a Saturday afternoon. I'd just done her weekly shopping. She was complaining that I'd bought the wrong brand of canned beans. She insisted on getting a can from her pantry in the basement to show me—why did she need so many damned beans?—even though I said I *knew* what brand she liked, but those ones had been on sale. I told her not to go down—that with her cane, it was dangerous; that if she really wanted me to see a stupid can of beans, I could go down myself, but she ignored me and pulled the door open and took the first step, and I *saw* her teeter, I swear I did, didn't I? And I reached out to grab her—that's what I did, what I *must* have done—but I was too late and down she fell, thumping the whole way—I'll never forget that sound—and at the bottom, curled up and holding her bleeding head in her hands, she died.

I told the police and paramedics all of it when they came. Then I had to call Troy, and tell him. The same story, again and again: I tried to grab her. She fell. I tried to grab her. She fell.

It was awful.

And though months had passed, it still kept me up at night—remembering that noise, *thump thump thump*, thinking about how trying to grab someone felt an awful lot like pushing them.

But of course, I didn't push her. I *couldn't* have. I didn't think I could have. I could have thought I didn't...

The car horn honked.

"Hey!" Troy yelled. "You coming or what?"

"Be right there!" I called back, forgetting, mostly, our argument.

I reached down to pluck the denture from the seeds and goop. I hated the way it felt in my fingers, sort of sticky and wet, but I didn't want Troy or the boys to find it.

I shoved it into my pocket.

Before I turned to go, I leaned down and whispered *"I know what you're doing. Stop it."*

In October, Troy got one of his ideas.

"Let's pick all Mom's pumpkins and make pies!" he said. "You can use her recipe instead of yours, honey."

"Yeah!" said the boys.

He smiled. "It'll be perfect," he said. "A perfect tribute, you know? To mark the anniversary."

"Sure," I said, my voice flat, but of course he didn't notice. "Perfect."

The next day, he and the boys drove to the cemetery to pick the pumpkins and clear away the vines so Burt wouldn't have to do it. I didn't go with them; I said I needed to get the kitchen ready, look through the pantry for the other ingredients.

But I knew where all the ingredients were. I kept an organized pantry: baking supplies were shelf three, right side.

When they got home, Troy pulled a bushel of squash and gourds from the trunk, and each of the boys carried a pumpkin so big their arms didn't reach all the way around. They were laughing, yelling for me to come see, saying Nanny gave them presents.

What could I do? The boys and I made the goddamn pies—three of them. Canned the squash, decorated the front porch with the rest.

When no one announced finding any more surprises hiding inside them, I relaxed. Maybe the brooch and the denture had been flukes—the casket not quite sealed, rainwater flooding in, items floating out and up.

It was less far-fetched than a curse. Even if I *did* push her a little that day, which I definitely did not. Ghostly harassment? That was just crazy.

And the pies were good. We ate one, gave the second to Old Burt, and froze the third to save for Thanksgiving.

It was our turn to host the holiday. My cousin and his family were supposed to come, but a snowstorm canceled their flight. My sister's youngest caught tonsilitis, so they stayed home, too.

That left the four of us with enough food for 12 people and a quiet house. Troy missed his mom. The kids were disappointed about not seeing their cousins. I was sympathetic, but drank too much wine anyway.

Maybe if I'd stayed sober, I could have seen what was coming. But, tricked by the coziness of my own home, I felt safe. Content, even, just me and my guys.

So after a quiet dinner, I shooed them all outside, asking Troy to help them build a snowman or make a fort or whatever. It gave them something to do and left me in peace to load the dishwasher the way I liked it.

That was my plan. But first, I sat down to finish the rest of the merlot and have another piece of pie. Troy was right about his mother's recipe being better than mine, though I wouldn't tell him that.

I slapped whipped cream onto the side of my plate, then held my wine glass up in a toast to her.

"Gone more than a year," I said to my empty kitchen. "Troy and the kids miss you a lot. Someday, probably, I'll miss you, too."

I took a bite. Cinnamon and cloves, pumpkin and vanilla. Heavenly. I took another bite, and another.

I downed what was left in the glass and shoved the last forkful of pie into my mouth, including the thick, buttery crust.

I chewed and swallowed.

Tried to swallow.

Something stuck in my throat—lodged there like a pebble, gluey chewed pie crust stopped up with it. I tried to cough it out; no use. It wouldn't go down or up. I couldn't holler for Troy and he wouldn't hear me anyway. I couldn't breathe—I panicked. Where had I left my phone? Wasn't there a way to do the Heimlich maneuver to yourself? Slamming your body against a chair, something like that? I stood up, desperate and willing to try anything, but I was too late, already. I couldn't save myself.

My lungs tried to suck in air that wasn't coming.

I didn't want to leave my boys. They were so little. They needed me—Troy too. Tears streamed from my eyes.

I fell to the floor and clutched at my neck. My vision clouded over; I saw my kitchen through a haze that got darker and darker.

And I knew, just then, what I was choking on.

Small and round. Like a pebble. Like a gumdrop.

What should have been in my mother-in-law's coffin, decorating one of her dead, rotting ears.

Formed in an oyster, grown in a pumpkin, baked in a pie: a freshwater pearl.

Half of the pair I'd always wanted. But not like this.

My chest spasmed. The pain was like a hot coal burning through me. I'd never thought about how much dying would hurt, or about how very powerless I'd feel—just a clump of flailing, doomed cells. I was no different than the pumpkin I'd stomped on at the cemetery: alive one...moment but not...the next...

My chest went still.

The pain stopped.

For my funeral they put me in my least favorite suit—a puke yellow that had *always* given me the pallor of death—and a silk scarf that didn't match, to hide my mottled neck. The mortician had feathered my bangs instead of sweeping them to the side, and as a last act of love, my husband pinned that awful brooch to my lapel.

I watched it all, my consciousness always hovering high above and to the left of whatever was going on, like I'd bought a cheap seat from which to view my own afterlife.

When the church service ended—nice, but the organ hadn't been tuned—they closed the casket lid, drove me to the cemetery, and buried me right next to my mother-in-law.

It was the last week of November. The mourners wore scuffed and dirty snow boots with their dress clothes. They stamped their feet and seemed thankful when the pastor cut the prayers short.

They left, but Troy and the boys remained: hands clasped, heads bowed.

"It's what Mommy would have wanted," said my husband—my *widower*—after a few moments. The boys sniffled, wiped tears and snot on coat sleeves I couldn't wash. "To be together with Nanny, forever and ever. That I'm sure of. That I know."

Henry nodded, so Noah did too.

Then they turned and walked away, leaving me alone with my fate.

A cackle sounded from somewhere next to me. I couldn't see her, but I knew that laugh.

"Got your *just desserts*, didn't you, dear?" she said, laughing anew at her pun.

Ugh. "*No.*"

"Yes! Oh yes. It's you and me, dear. You and me. Forever and ever, like my baby boy said." I could picture her smiling.

"*Baby boy*? He's 43, Bobbi."

"Still jealous of our relationship, I see," she said. Her voice had an annoying echo to it, like her words hit and then burrowed.

I'd have put my head in my hands, but I didn't seem to have hands anymore. Or a head.

"This can't be happening," I whispered. But I wasn't talking to her.

"That's what *I* thought," said Bobbi. "The day you *pushed* me down the stairs."

"You fell."

"You pushed."

"You *fell.*"

"Killer!"

"Bitch."

"Bitch!"

"*Bitch.*"

I wished I could cry. I wished I had a body to throw on the ground, feet to kick at the dirty slush.

But I only had this: me and Bobbi. Floating here, together.

No more stairs to push her down; no more hands to push her with.

Forever and ever.

LET THE BLACK DOG IN

(SOONER OR LATER, A WOMAN MUST MOURN)

The huge black dog showed up Friday evening, after her father's funeral.

Mira hadn't slept in days. Had barely eaten.

Wednesday morning, when the doctors at St. Luke's had told her it was time to let him go, she did. She signed the forms they told her to, then kissed her dad on his papery cheek. A nurse turned off the ventilator. Mira didn't cry. She called her brother. They waited, together, for his body to finally quit. Then she drove home.

She didn't cry at the wake on Thursday, either, and she didn't cry Friday afternoon, when pallbearers lowered her father into the graveyard soil baked dry by a month of hot July sunshine. Her brother gave the eulogy. She bowed her head, threw a rose down onto her father's casket when it was her turn.

She left the cemetery.

But back home, too tired to take off her funeral suit and propped on the couch like a doll put away, Mira heard it: panting that gusted like a hurricane. Footsteps that shook the ground.

Its fur blotted out the fading sun. Blocked the rising moon. Then the stars.

She listened, trembling, as the huge dog whuffed around the chimney and the second-story window frames. Then it sniffed the foundation, pawed at the front door, stuck its tongue through the mail slot.

When she wouldn't come out, it howled and howled, louder than a foghorn and twice as forlorn.

The siege continued throughout the weekend, then longer. Mira lost count of the days.

She hid in her bed, curling her body into itself like a mollusk. She squeezed her eyes shut. She covered her ears.

Pretending not to hear it didn't make it go away.

When she finally let it in, she was surprised by how it shrunk; by how easily, once she beckoned, it fit through the door.

SUFFER WITH THE TREES

(A LONELY NEWLYWED LEARNS THAT NATURE DOES
NOT FORGIVE AND DOES NOT FORGET)

Charlotte noticed the door in the hillside the Tuesday Edgar was supposed to be home but wasn't. He'd been expected that morning, but called to say he needed a few more days in the city.

Days away from his new wife and the cavernous new house he hadn't even slept in yet.

"Fine," she'd said, but she couldn't keep the strain from her voice. "I'm still settling in anyway. I'd hate for you to come home to stacks of packing crates."

And her husband had laughed and said "That's my girl," and Charlotte thought she'd heard another man's laugh too, but Edgar had already rung off, so she couldn't ask about it. Maybe it had just been an echo, or a bad connection.

Bad connection.

She'd lied. The house *was* set up. Swept and polished and aired while she waited for Edgar the way a kenneled dog waits for its master. Hoping for a walk and a head scratch.

Restless before 9 a.m., Charlotte finished her coffee and pulled on an old pair of Edgar's walking boots. She topped her apron with her stained house cardigan, put the roast back in the refrigerator, and went outside to explore the grounds.

There had been a hobby farm on the property, once upon a time. Charlotte crossed from the backyard into wilder grasses, fields that used to grow more than weeds and molehills. She could see old fence posts marking out a pasture for animals long gone, and a tumble-down shed that likely held rusted garden tools. She wondered if there was anything usable inside—she'd like to start a vegetable patch in a month or two, when the soil was good and warmed.

Nothing would grow in March, she knew.

She walked on and on. Her legs got sore and she liked the feeling. Better than sitting, idle, in the house her world had shrunk to.

The sun rose higher in the gray-blue sky.

A mile farther, maybe two, round a bend and past a stand of unwieldy scrub bushes, she saw it, but only because a flutter of wings near the ground drew her eye.

A door in the hillside, leaning back, made of plank wood lashed tight by frayed rope.

A passage from a forgotten school lesson came to Charlotte's lips, unbidden and too loud: "Over hill, over dale, through bush, through briar, over park, over pale, through blood, through fire..."

Who put a door in a hill?

She took a step toward it and stopped, remembering what Edgar had said to her last week when she'd asked about his business trip: "Curiosity killed the cat." She'd replied, "I'm not a cat, Edgar." And he'd said, "Even so."

Even so.

She crossed the grass and pawed away a fringe of creeping jenny to find a loop-wire handle. Unfastening it, she pulled. The rotting door cracked from the pressure but groaned open, revealing a dark hole with rounded sides of packed, smooth dirt.

And steps, leading down.

Curiosity...

She would just take a step in. Maybe two or three.

...killed the cat.

She'd just see what it was. What was there.

After 10 steps, then 12, Charlotte lost the daylight behind her.

She fumbled in her apron pocket until she grasped the box of kitchen matches she kept there. She struck a light and found herself looking at a low-ceilinged storeroom.

A root cellar. Of course.

A working farm would need a cool, dry place to keep potatoes and carrots, and there, in front of her, were the leavings—a bushel with mummified produce still inside, a shelf carved into the earth lined with dusty jars and bottles. Chipped crocks and beer steins in the corner. A wooden crate of what may have been turnips. A basket of plump red apples.

Apples. Plump and red. Fresh.

Fresh?

The match burned low and singed Charlotte's fingers. She threw it down and struck another. There the apples sat, shining.

The door behind her, at the top of the steps, banged closed. She jumped, dropping her match. It went out.

Feeling silly, telling herself she was nothing but a silly woman, a silly hungry woman—how long had she been away from the house? Breakfast was ages ago—she lighted another match.

Her fingers shook. She held them steady with her other hand.

She was hungry. That was all.

Was it?

The apples were plump and red and shiny and—she reached out and took one—firm.

Not soft and rotten like they should be.

Should be? They could have been put up a month ago, for all she knew. Two months. Root cellars keep. That's what they're for.

But where are the apple trees?

They could be a pasture over. Maybe two.

It's March.

Charlotte was hungry. She bit, and the match went out.

She dropped it and searched her apron for another. The box was empty. That didn't stop her from biting into the apple again and again. Its flesh was crisp and tangy. Sweet enough but sharp, too, like an autumn morning. Juice ran down her chin and she wiped it away with the sleeve of her sweater, turning and shuffling toward the steps in the dark.

Charlotte bumped the toes of Edgar's worn boots up the stairs and pushed against the wooden door with the flat of her hand. It barely moved. She put her half-eaten apple in her apron pocket to use both hands, and heaved.

The door opened and she climbed out.

Into an orchard so vast the rows stretched past the edge of the horizon.

Charlotte spun in a slow circle. What she saw didn't make sense.

Was there another entrance to the root cellar? Had she come out on the other side of the hill somehow—a trapdoor, a tunnel head? She must have gotten turned round in the dark, and with matchlight only, she couldn't have seen every corner.

If that was what happened, she told herself, and it must have been, all she had to do was find the entrance she'd gone in through and make her way from there back to the house—past the scrub bushes, back round the bend, past the garden shed and across the pasture and then up the porch steps and in through her own back door.

That's all she had to do.

That's all?

That's it. She just had to point her feet and walk.

Through miles of orchard.

It couldn't be miles. It was an illusion—a trick of the eye, of a tired mind. And it was getting on dusk, harder to see, harder to make things out in the—

Dusk.

How did it get so late?

Curious little cat.

"Shhhh" she said out loud. She wrapped her sweater tight across her chest to ward off the air's chill, chose a direction, and walked.

And walked. Walked and walked. Her feet were sore, the dusk didn't change, nothing round her seemed to change. Trees loaded with fruit, bark like scarred gray skin, rows upon rows, close and far away, a sylvan maze.

Was she going in circles?

She wished Edgar would have come home. She wouldn't have run off to explore, she wouldn't have gotten lost, if he'd just come home like he'd said he would.

But he hadn't wanted to.

He'd wanted to stay in the city, with the man who'd laughed so close to the phone.

How close?

She kept walking.

Hours passed. Charlotte wondered why it wasn't fully dark yet. She'd been walking so long blisters formed on her heels, but still the light stayed purplish and dim, stretching the trees' shadows like spiderwebs across her path.

And still she walked.

Her stomach growled. She remembered the apple in her apron and pulled it out. Something shimmered among its bitten flesh, undulating, and Charlotte held it closer, squinting.

Worms.

Pale maggots, their searching little bodies wriggling blind. Lolling. One fell and rolled down Charlotte's bare wrist. She shrieked and threw the apple, wishing, harder than she had all evening, that she was home, in her own kitchen, home and safe, all the lights burning away the nighttime. A panic took her, electrifying her tired legs.

She ran.

She had no better sense of direction than before. Low branches slapped at her. Twigs scraped her face, caught at her skirt and apron like bony hands, tore the fabric. Edgar's boots slowed her down, too big on her feet, clunking with each footfall, rubbing painfully against her blisters and tearing them open. Still, she ran on, ignoring her tears, down a row and cutting right—if she just kept cutting right, she had to end up at the old farm. Before long, she told herself, she'd see the house, or at least the garden shed. It would be alright. If she just kept running.

Keep running.

But she tripped, pain shooting up her leg from the knee that landed first against something hard. There was a dull crunch, maybe her kneecap, and what would she do if she couldn't walk? Would Edgar come home soon enough? Would he come searching for her?

But looking down, she saw it wasn't her kneecap that had crunched; it wasn't her bones at all, any of them, it was—

Bones.

She screamed.

She'd tripped over a body, lying in her path, propped halfway against one of the trees, its clothing in tatters. She screamed again, and it ended in a wail of self-pity. She choked on a sob and took a deep breath, wiping her face and scooting farther away from the corpse.

She couldn't snuff out the urge to look at it, and moved a little closer, careful not to touch it. Her eyes moved from detail to detail rather than taking in the whole.

The fashions it wore were decades out of date: a 1930s suit, boxy shouldered and double breasted. A ratty silk tie circled a neck of stretched-taught chords. The desiccated flesh looked like the vegetables in the root cellar: starved and concave, dried out. Its jaw flopped open and hung to the side.

A hand grabbed Charlotte's arm.

This time, the scream stuck in her throat, cutting off her airway. The dusky orchard and everything in it went black.

She came to with a man who wasn't Edgar waving a rank fedora in front of her face. She coughed and tried to push herself backward, away from him, but another one of those damned apple trees was right behind her.

"Who are you?" Charlotte asked, still in a half-faint. Her lashes fluttered. Was she dreaming? But strangers couldn't be in dreams, could they, and she'd never seen this man before. His suit was torn and filthy and his hair was a mess, cut at odd angles and different lengths, with a patchy beard to match. A wide gash beneath his left eye looked infected.

"Well that's some luck!" said the man. He sat back and put his hat on. "Marty already cashed in. If some broad showed up just to die on me as soon as I found her, well…"

"Marty?" she asked. Her head hurt.

The man pointed to the dead body. "That's Marty. And you're…"

"Charlotte."

"Wish I could say it's nice for you to meet me, Charlotte."

He held out his hand—that was grubby, too, with dirt-caked fingernails—and feeling, once again, like none of it could be real, not the place, not the man—Charlotte took it.

"Um. It's nice—I mean, how do you do…"

"Carl."

"Carl."

He held onto her hand and pulled her to her feet. "Say, you alright?" he asked, glancing down at her torn stockings and ripped dress. "The trees had a field day with you, I see."

The trees…

Charlotte whirled to look behind her, banged knee protesting, the pain proof of her wakefulness. But the trees stood silent in their grim rows, gray-skin bark and heavy branches unmoving. She turned back to Carl.

"Where am I? I need to go home—I have a house, not far from here, there's an old hobby farm, I just went down into the root cellar, just for a few minutes, it couldn't have been longer, and then I came out and—"

"And you were here."

"Yes. But *where*?"

Carl laughed. It was bitter. He kicked at the ground with a scuffed shoe, then spread his arms. "The orchard!"

Charlotte was tired and sore and hungry. Blood dripped from her knee. She was standing next to a dead body, and had no patience for mean jokes made by bizarre strangers.

"Fine," she said. "How do I *leave* it? I want to go home."

"I want to go home, too, doll," said Carl. "In fact, I've wanted to go home for... What year is it?" He stared past her head, into the distance.

"1962..."

How could he not know the year?

He shifted his focus back to her. "Then I've wanted to go home for over 20 years."

He laughed again, guffawed, but it turned into sobs. They wracked his thin body and he crumpled to the ground, wrapped his arms around his knees, and wept. Charlotte didn't know what to do. The man clearly wasn't well. Twenty years?

It couldn't be.

She was scared, but took a tentative step forward and reached down to pat his shoulder. "There now," she said. "It can't be as bad as all that. We're just lost. We'll find our way out of the orchard."

And the dead body?

She couldn't think about that. Wouldn't. She only had room for one thought: Get home.

Maybe Carl killed Marty.

Charlotte froze, then slowly straightened. Worse than being lost was being lost with a killer for company.

Carl stopped crying and looked up at her. Tears had streaked the dirt on his face into thin mud.

"Find our way out of the orchard?" he repeated. "I don't think so, doll. The orchard doesn't exist. It's not *here*."

"What?" she said. If this wasn't a nightmare it had to be a bad joke. "Stop it."

"Stop what?" said Carl, getting louder. "I'm telling you the truth! The orchard hasn't been here since Marty cut it down in '36!"

His eyes blazed and his face sweated and Charlotte backed away. Her own tears fell fresh and fear once again kicked at her chest, telling her to move.

Run.

She did. This time heading left, down a row, left again, always seeing the same trees, the same pattern, trapped in a carnival funhouse.

Too soon, her lungs heaved and her legs failed her. She couldn't keep running. Scratches on her neck were bleeding; a twig had caught and ripped out some of her hair. Her knee hurt and her side cramped and nausea soured her stomach. She slowed to a walk, made another left and—

"No," she whispered.

It was Carl, hands in his pockets, leaning against one of the trees. The remains of Marty lay against the base of the next one over.

Carl looked up. The fevered gleam had gone from his eyes. Exhaustion took its place. "I'm sorry," he said. "You believe me now?"

Charlotte nodded and sunk to the ground, stretching her sore legs in front of her. "I'm sorry for running away," she said. "This place, it's—I'm sorry." Her apology was inane. Idiotic.

"No skin off my nose," said Carl, apparently taking her flight from him, her fear of him, in stride. "And hey, you think I haven't tried to get away from *him*?" He nodded toward Marty. "I walk and I walk and then I turn and there he is. God, I'm sick of his mug. Alive or dead, I'm sick of his mug. This is all his fault." He looked at Charlotte's bleeding knee. "Hold still." He took a pocketknife from his suit coat and crouched down.

"Marty's? How?" She winced as Carl prodded the wound on her knee with the knife tip and flicked out, one at a time, three embedded pebbles. He stood and put his knife away. She thanked him and used her sweater to staunch the bleeding.

"Well—it's Marty's fault and mine. But really, we were just doing what we thought we should, you know?"

Charlotte shook her head. Of course she didn't know.

"The New Deal? Remember that?"

She shook her head again—she'd just turned 21—and Carl smirked, like it was the response he wanted. He straightened up and cleared his throat, then posed like a bad actor making too much of community theater.

"The AAA—the Agricultural Adjustment Act," he said. "The Depression wiped everyone out—all of us—but it hit farmers hard. And 'hobby farm,' you called it? After the market crashed, this was Marty's only bread maker."

"Wait—Marty owned my house?"

"Try to keep up, doll. Yeah, he did. But old Uncle Sam, he said let the crops go to rot. Force scarcity, drive up the prices. Shit. What a crock!" He spread his arms wide—another pose—like he awaited her applause.

She didn't give him any. He shrugged and kept going with his history lesson performance art, droning on, enjoying himself, gesturing and pacing back and forth between two of those horrible trees.

Charlotte thought he hadn't heard his own voice in a long time. But she didn't feel like humoring him and cut him off.

"What does that have to do with *now*?"

He turned on her, fists clenched. "*What does that have to with*—Jesus, let me finish!"

Charlotte threw her hands up—an instinctive defense against his changing moods—but he stepped back and cleared his throat again. For her safety, she needed to be a good listener. She sat up straighter and folded her hands in her lap.

Carl smiled and went back to his script: "As I was saying—Marty, he let the orchard go to pot, then, in '36, the AAA was ruled out; they said it was no good, and FDR, he told the farmers, he sent *us* to tell the farmers, and that meant *me*—yeah, government errand boy, here," he paused to snort, a stage laugh for his captive audience of one, then continued, "to go ahead and plant again, alfalfa or clover. Get those fields back in shape, and we'd dole out the subsidies." Carl mimed handing out money, flicking his wrist. "So Marty pulled out the struggling trees, put down the seed, and waited for payday." He folded his arms across his chest.

Charlotte wondered if the scene was over. If Carl would bow.

No. Not over yet, but winding down.

"Would you believe it, though?" he said, no longer peacocking. His shoulders drooped and his voice broke on his next words: "It wouldn't grow. The clover, it just wouldn't—and I walked the farm with Marty, he showed me the empty field, then we came by the root cellar, that goddamn root cellar, *shit*, this place, this cursed forsaken fucking *place*, it messes with you, it—"

He faltered, getting angry again. She brought him back to his story: "So this orchard—"

"Like I said. It. Doesn't. *Exist*."

He panted. Sank to his knees, then sat back and closed his eyes.

"Because Marty cut it down."

"Marty cut it down."

But...

"How are we in it, then?" she asked, feeling safer now that he wasn't standing over her. "These trees, they're here, I see them, they *touched* me." She reached out and slapped a trunk. "That's real."

The tree she hit seemed to shudder and twist. Its branches shook. Her hand stung where rough bark had grazed her palm and she pulled it back, held it to her chest.

Carl's eyes flew open. "Don't do that," he said. "Don't mess with the trees. Ever."

"What?"

"Marty there did. Tried to snap off a branch to start a fire. The trees broke his leg. You can see it, if you want. Just pull off his trousers. Left leg, below the knee."

There was no way Charlotte was going to undress a corpse. She stayed where she was.

"But the trees couldn't have..."

"Couldn't they?" Carl leaned closer. He pulled his soiled collar away from his neck, showing her a thick white scar. "I made the mistake of trying to climb one. I broke a few twigs, trying to find my footing. I just wanted to see if there was anything beyond the orchard."

"And was—"

"You think I made it to the top? That tree looped a branch into a noose and dropped me. Some days I wish it hadn't let me go."

"Oh God." Charlotte moved farther away from the tree she'd struck, picturing Carl swinging, strangling, legs kicking. But moving away from one tree brought her closer to another. They seemed to be closing in, blocking what little light there was. But trees moving, trees attacking, that was—

"Impossible," she finished aloud.

"Think so? Then you think wrong. This orchard can do whatever it wants," Carl said. "As happy as I was to see you—to see another person, I mean—I was sad, too. For you. The trees got themselves another trophy."

Charlotte shook her head. She couldn't accept it.

And yet...

Another thought struck her. "How are you alive?" He'd been here over twenty years, he'd said. Why wasn't he lying dead with Marty?

"Cellular respiration," Carl said. He took his hat off and scratched his head. "That's how."

"Sorry?" She hoped he wouldn't jump into another long soliloquy. He didn't.

"Cellular respiration. It's like the root cellar. Decomp slows down under the right conditions. I'm suspended, almost. Not really alive, just...not dead. Somewhere in between."

"And you're saying that now, now *I'm...*"

"Suspended, too."

Stuck.

"Not alive," she said. "Not dead."

Trophies.

"Afraid so. But see, Marty—he didn't want to be stuck anymore. He'd had enough of the orchard after it mangled his leg. He stopped eating—punched his own ticket. He told me I should do the same, but..."

"But what? Why didn't you?"

"I might, still. I just haven't yet. I keep eating these goddamn wormy apples, cooling my heels here like a picked vegetable, wondering if maybe... Well. Maybe I'll find a way out. I mean, you came in, so...?"

He looked at her as if she could help him, his face open and raw, hoping, clearly, that she had an answer he didn't.

She had nothing.

Charlotte shook her head and raised her shoulders; a helpless gesture.

Helpless.

Carl's face closed. He dropped his chin.

"Well then," he said.

A few tears she hadn't yet cried crept down her face. She wondered if she'd somehow done this to herself. She'd wished for a different life, hadn't she? A different life from the one she had with Edgar. And now here she was—a different life, a different man, and stuck just the same.

Carl reached forward, picked up a half-rotted apple from the ground, and held it out to her. "Here you go. Welcome to the orchard, Charlotte."

She looked at the apple. As she stared, a thick maggot broke through the fruit's bruised skin, probing the surface, tasting the air.

She retched. "No," she said, when she could speak. "I'll get some from one of the trees, I'll pick—"

"Don't," he said. "Don't ever pick fruit still hanging from the branches."

She pictured Carl dangling again, fighting for breath, the agony of it. "Okay," she whispered. She glanced at the apple he still held out for her. "But I can't—I can't it's..."

"You have to," he said. "It's the only grub here, the only way. Otherwise..." He gestured toward Marty with his chin. "Otherwise you're just...giving up."

Give up.

She looked at the apple, then at Carl. His ruined face. His ruined clothes.

"Please," he said.

Please.

"It's the only way."

The only way.

Carl smiled as she raised trembling fingers. She took the apple.

And threw it, hard as she could, into the darkness between the trees.

Then she sat down next to Marty, closed her eyes, and resolved to wait for the inevitable.

GHOST-KNOCKING

(MISCHIEVOUS BOYS FIND OUT PAYBACK IS A BITCH)

Colin was elected to do the knocking.

"Sorry, dude," said Nathan. "Majority rules."

The game was simple. Halloween night, go to their victim's house. Creep around it, knocking first on one side, then the other. Tap a stick against the windows. Lob rocks onto the roof.

Run away.

They couldn't have known that their teacher's elderly mother was home alone. That she'd be so scared she'd leave her bed, hurry down the stairs, lose her footing, bash her head.

It was the next night—each boy home, almost asleep—when the knocking started.

It's never stopped.

They lie awake and tremble.

MRS. ANDERSON, MRS. ANDERSON

Of course Sophie knew Neil's first wife had died in the house. She'd been the poor woman's night nurse.

What she didn't know, though, was just how long Mrs. Anderson would linger.

Sophie and Neil's love shocked the gossipy neighbors, his teenage children, her intolerant employers—but it was genuine, and began innocently enough.

Each evening, after the bedtime hospice routine—sponge bath, diaper, pajamas, medication—there hadn't been much more for Sophie to do. Night nurses were night watchmen.

And Neil—just 46, half a life still to live—was only human.

For four weeks he only came in and sat with Sophie: asking about Deborah's medications and doses, telling her about what a wonderful woman his wife had been before the cancer began to steal her away.

Sophie listened.

She was a good listener; end-of-life-care nursing had trained her for that. Always alert to heart rates and breathing patterns, the cry of a patient in the dim light of a sickroom.

"There was this one time…" Neil would start, and Sophie always said "Yes?"

Then story gave way to story, as stories always do: Sophie learned how much he worried for his kids—a daughter acting out and a son shutting down, how hard he'd worked to become an architect, how deeply it hurt that he could no longer care for his wife on his own.

But he wanted Sophie to talk, too, not just listen.

So she did.

She told him the job was making her lonely. She told him how her short marriage ended. She told him which songs made her sad, which ones made her dance; that she loved mustard but hated mayonnaise.

She talked, he smiled. He talked, she smiled.

Then, one night, his kids away at their aunt's for a break and Deborah sleeping fitfully, Neil suggested they give his wife some peace by moving into the living room downstairs.

They never made it.

As soon as they stepped into the hallway and closed the bedroom door, Neil caught Sophie's hand in his own and they clashed together like cymbals. He pinned her against the wall and she clutched at his backside; his lips moved along her neck.

It had been a long time since Sophie touched and was touched that way, a long time since she felt desirable to anyone at all. She moaned in pleasure and relief, and it drove Neil on. He spun her around, yanked down her leggings and dropped his own pants, wrapped his arm around her ribcage and thrust into her. She tried to keep her voice down when she said "Yes!," the word both consent and appreciation, a tiny prayer immediately answered. Neil finished inside her, then turned her to him and brought her to climax with his skilled artist's fingers.

A few moments of magic. A few moments of madness.

Directly afterward they pulled on their clothes. Sophie didn't know what to say and it seemed Neil didn't either. He looked confused, upset—like he'd break down crying. So Sophie took his hand and led him to the staircase, where they sat side by side, barely touching, and listened to the grandfather clock tick in the foyer below.

When—a half hour later, it couldn't have been more—Sophie went in to check on Deborah, she found her patient dead, head turned toward the door, her cooling brow creased and bloodless lips pursed.

Sophie had never seen a corpse make that face—usually the muscles went slack.

She tried not to let herself wonder if, even through the haze of morphine, Deborah had *heard*—if her last moments on this earth were filled with the sounds of her husband fucking another woman just outside the room in which she lay dying.

It was unthinkable.

So Sophie ran a hand over Deborah's face, smoothing it out, making her look peaceful, before she called Neil in to break the news.

The wedding was a quiet affair at City Hall.

They'd waited six months to marry, though Sophie's employers caught wind of their relationship and fired her after four.

She wasn't angry. The agency had a policy: no romance with the bereaved.

For another month after, they'd remained discreet; along with public image, there were the children to think of. Sophie never stayed over at his house, Neil never slept at her apartment.

"Soon," they'd tell each other. "Soon."

And that sense of waiting, their impatience during his mourning period, had been exquisite. It lent their daytime lovemaking a forbidden spice, feeling, a bit, as if he were still married and this was a torrid affair he snuck out for on his lunch breaks.

Sophie bought colorful lingerie in lace and satin and barely-there fishnet, forgetting her body image issues and her extra 15 pounds. Neil was always ready when she said "I need you," he whispered dirty words in her ears, swore she made him feel at least 10 years younger.

They fucked in every room of her apartment. One day, he even told her to get on her knees out on the balcony.

She did.

It was noon.

Their first night as husband and wife, a Friday, they had the house to themselves. The kids were once again at Neil's sister's, this time pouting and sulking. They hated Sophie and she understood why. "Give them time," Neil said, and she answered "Of course."

She meant it.

But that night, she didn't want to think about Neil's kids—her stepkids. She just wanted to enjoy her status as the new Mrs. Anderson, the blushing bride of a successful architect, one who had designed his own home and made partner at his firm before he turned 40. She wanted to feel sexy and hopeful and cherished. She wanted to screw her husband in their big, soft bed.

So she told Neil to wait in their bedroom—not the room he'd shared with Deborah, the one she'd died in, but a slightly smaller one across the hall—and slipped into the bathroom, where she put on a sheer nightie she'd bought just for the occasion.

Walking out of the bathroom, a chill took Sophie, raising gooseflesh all across her naked skin.

An open window? But the hallway had none.

She shivered in the sudden cold.

But it hardened her nipples, too, making them stick out the way Neil liked.

She walked back into the bedroom and slowly spun around twice for her groom before he pulled her onto their bed and flipped her onto her stomach.

She made him pull the blankets over them. She was still so cold.

Saturday morning, Sophie woke up to Neil kissing her neck, his erection digging into the back of her thigh. She cooed and smiled and kissed his fingers; she backed up for him, lifted her ass so he could spear her like a wet cherry on a cocktail sword.

They writhed together, and after just a moment, Sophie touched herself, wanting to climax with her husband, to crash like waves against one another.

She loved him, she thought. And he loved her back. It didn't matter that his kids needed time to adjust, or that she was snubbed by the neighbors, or that she and Neil hadn't been asked yet to his partner's Memorial Day barbeque.

Life was perfect, she told herself, moving her fingers faster. *Perfect enough.*

She lifted her head to watch them fuck in the mirror over the dresser. Neil's eyes were open too, meeting hers in the reflection. She liked seeing him watch her.

"*Tell me you love me,*" she whispered.

He did.

"Tell me you love me and call me your slut. Say to me things your coworkers think."

Deborah never let Neil talk dirty to her. So Sophie made a point to ask for it.

"I love you," he said, so close he was grunting, *"my sweet little slut, my darling whore, my filthy hot angel who comes just... for... me!"*

The last word ended in a shout; he squeezed her breast as he finished—squeezed so hard it hurt—and her own climax rocked her body.

Aftershocks rippled through her as she held eye contact with Neil. She thought of that first night in the hallway, pressed against the wall—what they'd unleashed, and how much she liked it.

Then, in the second before her husband pulled out and threw himself back against the bed, Deborah's dead face took the place of Sophie's in the glass—brow furrowed, lips pinched.

Sophie cried out.

Neil kissed her neck, mistaking the cry for an encore request.

The face disappeared.

Sophie closed her eyes.

Early Sunday, Neil went for a jog and let Sophie sleep in. He was still gone when she woke up, so she rolled out of bed to take a shower.

While she lathered her hair she made a mental shopping list—she wanted new towels for this bathroom, something fluffier; and the tacky floral swag above the toilet needed to be replaced with a practical shelf. She was still adding to her list when she heard the bathroom door open. She smiled; Neil must have missed her.

"Honey?" she said. "You're going to wear me out!" She laughed.

He didn't reply, but a hand pushed the shower curtain in toward her. She laughed again.

"Aim lower!" she said, and moved her backside toward the hand. But it glided upward. "Okay, Mr. Anderson; you're the boss," she said. She pushed her right breast into the waiting palm and giggled, expecting Neil's usual nipple caress.

Instead the hand clamped down painfully and the fingers squeezed. Sophie gasped.

"Neil!" she said. "Stop it! That hurts!"

The fingers twisted. Sophie grabbed the shower curtain and flung it open, blinking fast, soap stinging her eyes.

The pressure on her breast let up.

There was no one there.

She didn't mention the incident to Neil. What would she say? How could she explain it? And did it even happen? Her breast felt sore and her nipple tender, but that could have been from their lovemaking session the day before.

As a healthcare worker, she knew that lack of sleep could do bizarre things to a person's psyche, and between the funeral and losing her job and the wedding and the move and her new role as a stepmom, Sophie had been worrying herself awake most nights.

Then there was the guilt she tried to ignore—guilt could lead to paranoia, paranoia to hallucinations.

Easy as that, she explained it all away. Still, that night, she told Neil she had a headache and went to bed early.

She didn't sleep.

Monday Sophie was nervous being in the house alone, though she told herself she was being ridiculous.

Neil was at work; the kids had gone right from their aunt's to school and wouldn't be home until the afternoon. To keep herself from dwelling on what happened or didn't in the shower, she loaded the dishwasher and did laundry. First she put in the bedsheets, then the towels, and last, she planned to run a cycle on delicate—clean all that expensive lingerie she and Neil loved to get messy.

She turned on the radio and hummed along to classic rock while she stripped the bed and later remade it; moved a few boxes of Deborah's things to the basement; unpacked the dishwasher; folded towels. It was past one by the time the washer finished its delicate cycle, and she wanted to get her nighties and thongs upstairs to hang dry in the bedroom before the kids got home.

She opened the washer lid and pulled out her purple lace bodysuit.

It was chewed to bits.

Dismayed, she reached for her sheer nightie.

Ruined.

Her red satin bra and thong set.

Ripped apart at the straps and sides.

A few tears fell as she made sure to grab every bit of fabric. Neil had loved this stuff on her. She knew she could buy more, but still, it seemed like such a waste.

She took her armload of gauzy scraps to the kitchen and tossed them into the garbage, throwing an old newspaper on top of them so the kids wouldn't see. She'd have to tell Neil about it later; ask him to look at the washer. If it was going to ruin everything they put in it, they'd have to get a new one.

Their first dinner as a family didn't go well.

Sophie burned the chicken and undercooked the potatoes. Though Neil bravely cleaned his plate, the kids barely touched theirs. When Sophie asked Neil's daughter to pass the salt, she told her to "Get fucked." Neil yelled. His son glared silently.

Sophie couldn't take it anymore. Calm as she could, she excused herself and walked upstairs to collapse on her bed, crying.

Neil came in a moment later and rubbed her back in slow circles. He waited until the tears had slowed.

"They'll come around," he said. "This is all new to them. But I did give them a talking-to—they have to *try*."

"They don't want to," Sophie said. "And I get why."

"Shh," Neil soothed, and he let her cry some more.

Tuesday night, Sophie found her expensive hand cream smeared across her nightstand. Someone had dragged their finger through it to spell out *HOMEWRECKER*.

She cleaned it up without saying anything to Neil. Let the kids get it out of their system—throw their tantrums while she stayed steady, a rock withstanding the current.

Wednesday, Sophie realized all the food in the fridge had spoiled. Another appliance failure?

Thursday, she discovered her makeup sunk to the bottom of the toilet bowl. Surely the kids.

Friday night, as she lay awake and Neil and the kids slept, every lightbulb in the house surged bright and then exploded. The kids were too scared to be mean to her; they just hovered in their bedroom doorways, wide eyed. Neil wondered if the neighbors had gotten the same electrical spike; Sophie said they must have. Neil said he'd call the power company Monday, told the kids to go back to sleep. He and Sophie cleaned up broken glass for the rest of the night.

He cut himself once.

She cut herself twice.

By mid-weekend, exhausted and anxious, Sophie admitted to herself that despite sleep deprivation and whatever mean pranks the kids *were* responsible for, she was still well and truly haunted.

She didn't tell Neil. She didn't say anything to the kids. Because sad as Deborah's story was, miss her and mourn her as the family deserved to and did, life was for the living and Neil and the house were *hers*. Fair and square.

But if Deborah needed help moving on, Sophie would help her.

If Deborah wanted to play dirty tricks, Sophie could play too.

And if Deborah thought she was the only woman who could ever make Neil happy, Sophie would surely prove her wrong.

She fucked Neil exuberantly Saturday night and Sunday morning, riding him hard while he called her every name in the book. She listened, delighted; watching in the mirror, daring Deborah to appear.

While he was at work on Monday, Sophie pulled down Deborah's ugly modern farmhouse decorations and threw them in a donation bin three blocks over.

She took Neil's and Deborah's wedding album from beneath the coffee table and shoved it in the bottom of the junk drawer in the pantry. It was going too far, she knew, but didn't care—she'd cross every line in the world for Neil.

But the activity, the worry, the lack of sleep was all catching up, so when Sophie finished purging the house in every way she could think of, she retreated to her and Neil's bedroom to maybe cry and definitely nap. She felt so tired it was difficult to move her heavy limbs up the staircase. When she made it to her room, she crawled under the covers and drifted off in seconds.

She woke to whispers.

At first she thought it was the kids, home from school, talking downstairs. She looked at the bedside clock—only noon. Not the kids.

She shook off her grogginess, listening harder: a woman's voice, harsh whispers, like a mother scolding her kids in church.

Like a dead wife cursing her replacement.

Sophie was so frightened that she found it hard to breathe. She curled into a ball and trembled, wishing Neil or even the kids would come home early. Anyone so she didn't have to be there, alone, hearing what she did.

Most of the words were indistinguishable, but now and then, breaking up a stream of angry mutterings, Sophie could make out the word *mine*. Hot tears soaked her pillow. She tried to wait it out. But when it seemed like the voice would never stop, she whispered back, blubbering through snot and saliva and tears.

"Please," she said. "Please, leave us alone." The whispers intensified. "I'm sorry about that first night—we didn't mean for it to happen, I swear, but it *did* and we fell in love—"

A cackle made Sophie stop.

It echoed in her head.

She shoved herself back, trying to get closer to the headboard, to protect herself.

From what? A voice?

She took a deep breath and reminded herself, again, that this was *her* house. That *she* was Mrs. Anderson, just as legitimate as Deborah had been.

Had been. Past tense.

She sniffed, wiped her eyes with the sheet. Sat up straight in bed, and spoke calmly, her voice only wavering a little.

"Deborah," she said. "I know you're here. I know you still love Neil. And part of him will always love you. But it's time for you to leave, move on. You can't scare me away. I'm not going anywhere."

Then, just by her ear, so close she could feel the puff of breath and smell its staleness: *"Neither am I."*

So.

It was to be a war of attrition.

Days and then weeks and then months passed. The whispers came and went. Drains clogged and birds flew into windows. The sex slowed down but stayed hot. Pictures fell and electricity failed. Sophie didn't look for a new job. The kids grew tolerant. Shoelaces knotted and rosebushes died. Friday nights became pizza nights. What broke was replaced.

Sophie loved Neil.

Neil loved Sophie.

Deborah stayed angry.

Sophie stayed calm.

The house stayed haunted.

Perfect enough.

The Hole Had Always Been There

(A GRIEVING TEENAGER MUST DECIDE WHETHER HE'LL FOLLOW HIS DEAD MOTHER INTO DARKNESS OR STAY TOPSIDE WITH HIS HOPELESS FATHER)

The hole in the retaining wall had always been there, as far back into the *before* as Davey could remember.

The earth it held back sloped up and away from Davey's yard, rising into a hill.

Beyond the hill lay the cemetery.

Davey's mom was there now, and her *now* meant *forever*. She would *always now* be there, while he was stuck, helpless, in the *after*.

Hours after his mother's funeral, Davey stood near the retaining wall, hidden by the garage, smoking a joint he'd filched from his father. Not that his dad was likely to notice—neither Davey being gone, nor the missing joint—because Davey's father moved in a fog of grief and bewilderment and noticed nothing.

Davey was on his own.

He stared at the hole and tried not to shiver in the March wind. He was a *tough kid*—the term everyone seemed to be using for him, which, Davey knew, translated to *kid with a dead mom*.

But tough kids get cold too and Davey *did* shiver, huddling closer to the tight-packed stones that made up the retaining wall. Closer to the hole.

It seemed bigger than it used to be.

Was it the angle? Davey moved away—no. It *was* bigger, though *bigger* was a funny way to describe a hole. A hole was an *absence*; a hole was a *lack*, and the only thing Davey could think about now was what he lacked.

So thinking and brooding, trying not to shiver or cry, Davey wrapped his lips around the joint and sucked its skunky fire into his lungs. Thanks to eleventh grade health class, he knew all about weed's dangers: *naphthalene, acrylamide, acrylonitrile metabolites*. He whispered the names of the poisons and inhaled again. Like a magic spell, they rode the smoke into all the places within himself Davey could not see—dark empty places hollowed by grief—and filled them up.

He leaned forward and blew smoke into the hole in the retaining wall.

The hole blew it back.

Davey's eyes watered and stung. He coughed.

Then, curious, he stepped closer, looking for the source of the air current. Wind through a drainage pipe? Or an animal's den—a fox or raccoon, huffing Davey's smoke back and away?

Poking into the hole seemed dangerous—*foolish*, his mother would have said, but because she was dead and couldn't scold him about this or anything else ever again, that's what Davey did.

He put his hand in first, then his arm up to the elbow. Inside it was chilly and still. No wind moved, no animal scuttled. The space was large—larger than its mouth, though that was growing again, widening, as if the retaining wall was yawning. Davey heard the sound of rocks rubbing together. It made him think of cracking bones.

He knew holes shouldn't shift and grow this way. But he thought he'd known that mothers didn't fall down dead without warning. Here, in the *after*, Davey threw out the rules of the *before*.

He pulled his hand back and watched. The hole dilated. Loose dirt sifted down to the grass, dislodged by the heaving and grinding of the stones. Davey wondered if the wall would crumble—if the hill would come sliding down, burying the yard and the garage and Davey with them, rolling over him like a dark drowning wave of clammy earth.

He wondered if he would like it. He thought he might.

The sounds stopped.

The hole didn't get any bigger.

He measured the opening: longer than his forearm. If he squeezed through, he could crawl inside. If he crawled inside, the rest of the lonely motherless world would go away. And if the rest of the world went away, Davey could finally cry, as long and hard and hopeless as he wanted to, with no one else to hear him.

He went in.

As his final foot left the security of his lawn, though, Davey wondered if his father had eaten anything for dinner. He often forgot, and wouldn't eat unless Davey microwaved something and set it down in front of him—reheated casseroles left by the neighbors or Hungry Man frozen meals bought on sale.

It made him ache to worry about his dad, and he worried about him all the time.

He told himself he'd go in soon—but not yet.

The dirt he knelt in was soft, and Davey reached out with his right hand to explore the rest of his surroundings: damp earth and hair-thin roots. Here and there, a smooth pebble. The wriggling wet body of a night crawler he was careful not to crush.

The tip of his joint gave off no light. He pulled his knees up and moved into a sitting position.

He squeezed his eyes shut and told himself it would be fine to cry. He *wanted* to cry. He always wanted to cry. But he was tired. So tired that sitting seemed difficult. So he leaned back and stubbed out the butt of his joint, enjoying the way it hissed in the dirt, enjoying the way the dirt cradled his body.

Then he heard his father calling him from the back porch. His voice sounded raw; the second time he said Davey's name, it cracked.

Davey knew he should call back. Tell his dad he was okay; go to him, microwave something, sit next to him on the couch. Eat and pretend to watch TV and then go to bed, telling himself that if nothing else—and there was nothing else—they had each other. Or at least, Davey's dad had him.

He looked back toward his house; he opened his mouth to holler.

The hole's mouth shrunk.

Davey's throat tightened. He opened his mouth; the hole shrunk again.

He pitched himself forward to crawl out—he'd claw through if he had to—but a new sound made him stop.

It came from deeper within the hole—from deep within the place the hole led to—from shadows and root-twists and dankness and a breeze like warm breath: his mother's voice.

"Come here, sweetheart."

He heard her say it the way she used to when she needed him—to come in for dinner, to help her in the garden, to tell her about the book he was reading.

Hearing it again took all the oxygen from his lungs. He sat back.

"Mom?" he whispered.

Then a call from the other direction—his dad's voice: "Davey? Are you there?" Louder and closer. In the backyard now, shouting from the darkness near the rusted swing set he'd built for Davey more than 10 years ago.

Davey was torn.

He could smell his mother—plain Dove soap and rosemary sap.

"Honey?" she said.

"Mom," he said.

"Davey?" his dad called. A note of panic pitched his voice high: "Son!"

Was his mother humming? She used to—old songs Davey didn't know.

His chest tightened. He wanted to crawl out and he wanted to crawl deeper.

His mother's voice called him: "Davey!"

His father's voice called him: "Davey!"

He missed them both—his mother who was gone forever, his father who was gone too, in a different way.

His mother's voice called to him: "Come here, sweetheart."

His father's voice called to him: "Come on! It's late."

He loved them both. He missed them both.

He couldn't do it anymore.

The tight feeling in his chest gave way to a tearing; something inside pulled to the outside, like stuffing ripped out of a toy.

Davey went cold, then hot—a flush from the top of his spine to his heels. Bright, sharp pain, so quick he couldn't scream, gone just as fast, its departure like bubbles rising, leaving him dizzy.

Then, dreamlike, he watched himself frown, turn away, crawl toward the mouth of the tunnel, toward his father's voice. His head and then arms and then shoulders and waist and hips legs feet disappeared. He heard his dad's voice—he called him, the other Davey, "buddy." He said "There you are!" He said "Let's go inside."

And that Davey must have said a word like "yes" or "okay" or even a sulky "fine," because then Davey—the Davey still inside the hole—didn't hear anything more.

Until he did.

A different sound.

It was his mother's laugh—the delighted one, like when she won a game of Scrabble or knew the answer on *Wheel of Fortune*. The voice box in his own throat croaked out "Mom?"

The laugh again, like confirmation, like "Come closer."

So he yelled it: "Mom!"

He wondered if he was dead too.

He wondered if ghosts could feel sad.

He wondered if he should leave—hurry, catch up to his other self, stitch them back together, decide for good that *after* was better than *not at all*.

But: "Davey. Honey. Davey," his mother called. Quieter now. She was moving away from him—leaving him, again.

No.

He couldn't let that happen.

Without looking behind him at the hole that led back to his life, to his dad, to his grief—the hole that was maybe getting smaller even now, was maybe shrinking down to nothing and there'd be no undoing this, but Davey didn't care, he called again: "Mom!"

"Davey?" she said.

"Wait!" he said. "Mom…"

The tunnel wove through the dark, and he crawled and he crawled—this underworld Davey, this otherworld Davey, already so pale—he crawled to his mother and into her arms; her arms felt so cold, the cold chilled so deep; in the deep-dark they stayed and there they lay still.

Holding each other.

Always now and after.

DEAD MAN'S PIE

(JUST BECAUSE A STOLEN PIE WAS EATEN DOESN'T
MEAN IT CAN'T BE TAKEN BACK)

How was Jed to know the pie belonged to a dead man, or that dead men come back to claim what's theirs? When he walked by the Masons' farmhouse and saw that blueberry pie smelling like God's heaven cooling on a windowsill, he helped himself. Glenn Mason had fired him, unjustly, Jed swore, two days prior. That pie was his severance.

Except Jed couldn't know that Glenn had passed not 20 minutes earlier, tipped over from a blown heart while slinging hay bales, and that pie was his dear wife Annie May's last gift to him, one Glenn intended to bring along into the great hereafter.

Late in the night, Jed's former boss came for what was rightly his, and that the pie was already masticated in Jed's full belly didn't matter. Glenn's walking corpse, already smelling of carrion in the sun, woke Jed with a cuff to the ear. And though Jed screamed and kicked, he was no match for a man who'd been tougher than him living and was even more so dead.

Jed was found the next day, gut ripped open and empty, blue pie and red blood swirling into pulpy purple stains on his ruined bedsheets.

RESTORING THE EMPIRE REVIEW

On Friday evening, Barbara walked through the derelict Empire Review theater, thinking, again, that she could hear whispers coming from the balcony and the backstage wings.

Nothing distinct—never distinct, and surely her imagination, obsessed with the theater for so long that it became a living thing to her.

She strained to listen; the sibilant sounds faded, and all she heard was her own heartbeat, the whooshing of blood through her ears, breath held.

She let it out.

The Empire Review. Such a grand name for a place that had been left to crumble in one of Buffalo's most forgotten neighborhoods.

But it would fall no further.

Head of the Historical Preservation Society, Barbara had worked for the past five years, and finally, she'd done it: secured enough money to begin restoration of this Queen City gem.

The board had been hard to convince. But weren't they always? She'd stood before them in meeting after meeting in high-buttoned blouses and steel-gray pantsuits, the very picture of poise and fiscal logic, delivering her proposal:

If they brought back the Empire Review, it would jump-start a neighborhood renewal that would spread like wildfire, making the rust-belt city a waterfront tourist destination.

Now, in March of the year 2000, it was finally happening. Permits were signed. Funds were in the bank. Utilities had been turned on: water, gas, electric.

Work would start Monday.

Barbara ran her hand lovingly over the tattered upholstery of an aisle seat, like she was petting a favorite cat.

"We did it," she said aloud to the empty theater.

Again, the illusion: like the building responded to her.

She shook her head, blaming tiredness as she looked at her watch, then put on her coat.

Her footsteps echoed as she crossed through the lobby, its marble floors dirty but intact. Next she shut off the lights, murmured "Goodnight" and locked the door, and stepped out into the trash-strewn street.

Her happy sigh fogged the air around her like smoke.

Monday morning, Alan dogged her steps, like always.

He was a good assistant though—careful, meticulous. He kept the books, drew up the contracts, liaised with other city departments. He left her free to concentrate on what she loved best: the buildings. The way they used to be, or at least the way she imagined them. Sometimes, historical records proved a place's dignity. Other times, Barbara had to concoct it—give a building the past it deserved.

She never lied outright. She was a historian: truth was important. Just, perhaps, not *all* of it.

The little theater she'd fallen in love with had noble beginnings.

A community theater built in the early years of the twentieth century, it brought the flair of Europe to Buffalo: concerts and operas and dramas. But it failed in the late 1920s—the stock market crash didn't spare Buffalo—and became something less worthy of acclaim. A performance space for bargain-rate burlesque shows and foul-mouthed comedians, and downstairs—the board could never learn of it—a bordello.

Barbara had only learned herself through donated family documents—the woman's great-grandmother had been a performer, she'd found them in an old trunk, chittering like a squirrel to Barbara on the phone: *Aren't they fabulous? Look at those feathers! Those stage names! Lovely Letty and Sugarbum Sherly. A real find!* It had hurt Barbara to bury the photos and playbills in the back of her bedroom closet, but what else could she do? She'd never get a grant to restore a whorehouse.

There'd been a fire in '36. Omitting the nature of the costumes, the various states of undress of the performers, Barbara told the story during the tours she gave to potential donors and city officials. Everyone loved a tragedy.

"The fire started in the basement, in the dressing rooms," she'd say. "The records don't say what started it. Maybe cigarette ash, falling onto a starlet's gown. Maybe a knocked-over candle in a space without enough electric light. But whatever started it, the fire smoldered and filled the basement with smoke. The audience members, upstairs, along with the performers onstage, were able to get out. But anyone downstairs..." Here she would trail off, let the tour group listen for a moment to the theater's silence. "They died here."

"Can we go down there?" someone would always ask, eyes shining. Morbid fascination was present in every group.

"I'm sorry," Barbara would sigh. "Though the main floor of the Empire Review was mostly spared, the basement is in ruins. For safety reasons, we can't bring groups down there."

Then she'd give another fundraising push:

"It's your generosity and hometown pride that will allow us to restore the theater, including the basement's prop storage and dressing rooms. There's a jar in the lobby to help jumpstart our efforts; when you leave, if you'd be so kind as to drop in a dollar, we'd appreciate it so much."

Whenever Barbara said "we," she meant herself and the theater. Its seats and its aisles and its walls and its stage, a thing once alive, a thing she'd resurrect.

She never let herself think too long about its ghosts.

"Barbie? What do you say?"

Alan broke into her thoughts. She'd been staring at the ceiling, imagining the intricate whorls and leaf designs that she'd see soon enough, when the builders got to repairing the plasterwork.

"I've said before, don't call me that." It made her think of the boys in high school, the reputation she's earned when she wasn't careful enough. She smoothed the front of her blouse, making sure it was still tucked in tight, and turned to Alan. "Now what were you asking me?"

"Tonight? Drinks to celebrate?" She blinked at him. He raised his eyebrows. "Getting the grant, starting restoration?"

"Maybe another time," she said. Her usual answer to his many invitations. "Too much to do."

That night, Barbara got home to her apartment—a mansion-turned-flats on the west side—looking forward to a soak in her bathtub.

She peeled off her suit jacket and blouse, trouser socks and pleated slacks, and walked into the bathroom barefoot. She regarded herself in the vanity mirror—middle-aged skin, pale as usual this late in the winter, contrasted by her bra and underwear in black lace.

Like the theater, she had her own suppressed past. Dubbed "Boobie Barbie" as an Ohio teenager by the boys she'd let touch them, she'd become someone new in college. A serious scholar. Turtlenecks and French twists. President of the History Club. A bright future. Respect.

But beneath the tweed and herringbone, she was still a woman. A lonely one. She remembered that, sometimes—even got a little sad about it. But what was the alternative? Bars and singles clubs? Awkward blind dates set up by well-meaning friends? *Alan*?

No thank you. She'd rather be alone—though she wasn't, really. She had her buildings.

And they had her.

She slipped off her lace undergarments. In the bath, she was once again covered, this time by bubbles.

The rest of the week was almost euphoric.

Barbara stopped in at the theater each day, watched as damaged walls were opened up and mildew-stained carpets were torn out. Bit by bit, demolition was erasing the theater's shame and dark days. Its depravation. What was left would be clean and bare, ready for renewal. A future as bright as the Empire Review's first hopeful, glitzy years.

Another Friday night, and once more she stayed late. The workers had gone. Alan had been there, too, leaving only when Barbara practically shooed him out.

The seats were all in a state of disassembly, stripped of their old fabric and dry-rotted cushions, armrests removed. So Barbara turned down the house lights and sat on the edge of the stage, her feet hanging over the space where, way back when, a small orchestra would have played.

She closed her eyes: pictured red velvet seats, chandeliers, polished brass and two hundred and twenty-six sets of clapping hands.

"I can see it," she whispered.

"See us," a voice from behind her whispered back.

Barbara's eyes flew open and she jumped off the stage, spinning around as she did, trying to face whomever had snuck up on her in the dark.

She landed hard. Fell. Her left ankle twisted painfully, and she cried out.

No one answered this time. She blinked and her heart hammered. Alan had told her 20 times that she needed to get a cellular phone, but they were expensive and felt too modern, like something from a science fiction story. She should have listened to him; she could have called for help. She tried to stand, to put weight on her ankle; the pain shocked through her and she fell again. With groping hands, she collected her purse and coat from the edge of the stage, pulled the fabric over her shoulders and hitched her purse across her body so it dug into her armpit.

Without a phone to summon help she was forced to crawl, ruining her slacks, up the aisle and toward the doors that led to the lobby. It was slow, she had to avoid debris, and by midpoint, she decided she hadn't heard any voice at all—it was her mind playing tricks. Maybe it was the chemicals fogging her perception—wood stripper and paint thinner, hundred-year-old glue steamed loose when they removed the bubbled damask-style wallpaper.

At the lobby doors, she pulled herself up, and supporting her weight with a hand against the wall, limped to the main entrance. Out on the sidewalk, she pried her keys from her pocket. Just before she pulled the door closed, she thought she heard that voice again, following her into the night:

"See us."

She drove to the hospital's ER after she left the theater. Over the weekend, she rested and ignored Alan's calls. Took Monday and Tuesday off. Most of Wednesday, too. But late in the afternoon, around 4, bored and curious, she took a cab to the Empire. She wanted to see if the builders had closed up the walls yet.

They had, mostly. But she saw wood scraps lying in heaps: MDF. Pressboard. Engineered materials. Not what should be used in historical restoration—not what the contracts *mandated*.

Barbara's mind spun. What was this? Construction fraud? Cheaping out on materials to make a better profit? She'd call Alan. They'd have to fire the company. They'd already paid *thousands*. They'd have to take the contractor to court. What a mess.

She made her way to the stairs on stage left, dropped her crutches, and sat down to cry.

A few minutes later, the lobby doors swung open.

"Alan!" She dried her eyes on her jacket sleeve and sat up straighter. He didn't need to see her crumpled.

"Barbie?" he called. He had a plastic smile on his face. "Thought you were taking the day off."

"Well I was, but—"

"Didn't see your car," he said, walking closer, still with that frozen smile.

"I took a cab." He was making her uncomfortable. "We need to talk about these building materials, they're—"

"I know," he said. "That's why I'm here, too."

"Good!" she said, relieved. "Because—"

"I stopped in to clear away the evidence before you saw it tomorrow." He walked over to a pile of wood scraps and kicked it.

Realization made her heart pound. "Are you saying you knew about this? The contract..."

"The contract I wrote?"

"That money," she breathed. "Alan, it's for..."

"For your precious theater? Of course," he said. His voice was different. Louder, mocking. "But I'm just skimming a bit. I deserve it. I do so much for you. Ask for so little. A drink now and then. A date. A chance to—"

"Wait. Alan." She blinked, disbelieving. A shock on top of shock. "You're stealing funds because I won't go *out* with you? That's—"

"Fraud? Larceny?"

"*Sick.*"

He shrugged.

"You'll get caught. The inspection. And the *builders* know, they'll—"

"Keep their mouths shut, because they got paid." He laughed. "As for the inspection...like I said. I came to clean up evidence." He pulled a can of lighter fluid from his pocket and shook it. Barbara heard the liquid slosh.

Her mouth went dry. She tried to get up. Alan lurched forward, grabbed her crutches, and threw them across the stage.

"The thing with new materials. You know what's wrong with them, don't you, Barbie? You, with your love of old buildings. Dreary, dead old buildings and nothing else." He squirted lighter fluid onto a pile of MDF, along the floor, onto the seats behind him.

"No..." she said.

"Say it."

"They burn too fast," she whispered.

"That's right!" Alan said. "Smarty-pants. People used to have about 20 minutes to get out of a burning building. And now?" He waited.

She swallowed a sob. "Two."

"Two." He dropped the lighter fluid, took matches from his pocket.

"Please don't," she said. "Please."

"Shhh," he said. "Barbie. You had your chance. It's too late, now. For you and this shit-heap theater."

"Alan..."

"Too bad no one knew you were here," he said. "I'll cry so hard when they tell me. Bye now, Barbie."

He struck a match and dropped it. Flames raced and jumped. Alan's retreating figure disappeared behind a wall of fire.

She pushed herself back—up the steps, onto the stage. There was an alley exit back there—she just had to get to it.

The smoke turned black, got thicker. She coughed and crawled. No time to find her crutches. Her eyes streamed tears. She found the door and pushed.

It was stuck. Wouldn't budge. Had Alan wedged it shut?

She sobbed, beat her fists against it.

Then, above the crackling, voices. Whispers. Calling her name, from centerstage.

"Barbara. Over here. Hurry. This way."

She turned.

The trapdoor. It was open. Hands reached out: women's hands, women's bare arms. Barbara got closer; the hands grabbed, pulled her down, shut the door. In the dark, she could just make out their charred faces, counted six.

"Do you see us now?" rasped a woman with a red-painted mouth.

"Do you see us?" said a blonde with a black eye.

Barbara trembled, shivered despite the heat. It couldn't be real, yet there they were. The dancers. The dancers and sex workers who had died in the 1936 fire. The ones Barbara had lied about, erased from her stories. Erased from history.

Fear and smoke closed her throat, but she nodded. Her ankle throbbed. The women wrapped their arms around her and pulled her close.

They stood in a huddle, surrounding her. Their cold bodies protected her from the creeping heat, forgiveness in their embrace Barbara knew she didn't deserve.

"I'm sorry," Barbara mumbled. "So sorry."

They held her tighter. She buried her face in the collarbone of a redhead with soot on her cheeks.

"*Shhh, shhh,*" they hushed her, and the scent of their mingled perfume cut through the smoke. She tried to breathe them in—these women who'd lived and died, whose stories mattered.

She took one last, smoke-filled breath, and was gone.

She'd died, there beneath the stage.

The doctor explained it to her, once she was well enough to talk, when she was conscious enough to listen. He said it like it was no big deal—dying, coming back. Getting a second chance at everything.

"How long?" she wheezed. "How long was I gone?"

"Moments," he said. "Not more. Getting beneath the stage kept you from breathing in more smoke than you did. Smart. Then the EMTs brought you back in the ambulance. What do you remember?"

Barbara thought of the women. The ones who'd rescued her.

"I—" she started. How to explain? To say she didn't save herself? But she couldn't leave them out of any more stories. She took a shaky breath and said, "The women called to me. The dancers. They helped me."

"Dancers?" The doctor raised his eyebrows. Smiled. Told her the nurses would be in later.

He didn't believe her. Fuck him. He didn't have to.

Over the next several days, Barbara talked to police, to fire investigators, to city officials. Alan was gone, they told her. So were the funds from the Empire's accounts. But there would be a little money from an insurance policy Barbara had set up herself, and the theater wasn't a total loss—the interior walls had burned, and there was smoke and water damage, but the stage was intact and so was the lobby.

All Barbara heard was "salvageable."

She healed, gained strength, then got to work: she scheduled interviews with *The Buffalo News*, with Channels Two and Seven, with local magazines. She dug out the documents she'd stashed: Sugarbum Shirly was the redhead. Lovely Letty, the blonde with the black eye. Online searches and community pleas revealed the others: Lucy the Legs, Honey Lee, Saint Ira, Stella Star. She still needed most of their real names, but she'd find them. Birthdays, biographies. Favorite songs. Signature moves.

And when her research was complete, the fundraising would start. She'd call for help and Buffalo would answer. She'd rebuild the theater with her own hands, if she had to—using the right materials this time, of course.

Another Friday night. Mid-May, and springtime woke the city up. Buds on trees, all the dirty snow melted. A freshness to the air that made Barbara feel like skipping.

Instead, she unlocked the entrance to the Empire and stepped in. She turned on a work light and aimed it at the largest wall in the lobby—the one right between the twin doors of the theater.

She smiled, sketching it out in her mind, overlaying the water-bulged plaster with her vision: a memorial, their names in lights again, no more shame, no more hiding: *To the Women of the Empire Review*.

"I see you," she whispered into the shadows.

And soon, everyone else would, too.

ROCK-A-BYE

The moment the doctor said *stillborn*, Nora floated away.

She no longer saw the white-walled room, the scrub-clad nurses, the look of naked repugnance in Pete's eyes. She didn't hear the doctor ask her if she wanted to hold her lifeless baby. To say goodbye.

Two days later, when Pete drove her home from the hospital and helped her out of the car, Nora heard neither the gravel crunching beneath her slippers nor felt the biting January wind. She took no notice when, as she walked through a house that felt like someone else's, blood streaked down her legs and ran into her white cotton socks, pooling beneath her heels to stamp a trail across the carpet.

She got into the bed Pete said was theirs, and she didn't leave it until he made her—pulled her up, walked her to the shower, and turned on the spray.

There, she was forced to confront her treacherous body: a loose, empty stomach. Ankles still swollen. Breasts crusted with milk her dead baby didn't need.

She cried. Leaking, small tears and then gusty sobs that echoed against the tiled shower walls and buckled her knees.

By the time she emerged from the bathroom, in a soft robe with her wet black hair in a knot, her eyes were dry and she was once again quiet.

Nora saw the stranger in her yard a few days later: small, skinny frame, dark hair hiding her face. She disappeared through the gate in the back fence as Nora looked from her bedroom window, watching snow fall against the backdrop of a bleak, gray sky.

Someone taking a shortcut, maybe? Someone lost, going back how they came?

Snow fell. She watched it.

Behind their house on Old Main Road lay the town's cemetery.

In two days, they'd have the funeral there. Pete hadn't wanted to; he couldn't understand why Nora did. What was the point of putting herself, and him, through such a public display?

But Nora insisted. She threw a lamp, gouged the dining table, smashed a framed wedding photo; wept on the floor with her face in her hands.

Pete watched.

The clock ticked.

He relented.

They sat at the cluttered kitchen counter the night before the funeral. Pete ate sausage pizza while Nora tried to.

Their argument had resumed.

"Honey," he said, "I'm thinking of us. Of *you*. Is this really what we need? The cemetery's right *there*, for fuck's sake. How will we ever get away from this?"

Nora dropped her pizza slice, pushed her plate away. She stared at her husband in disbelief.

"Wait," she said. "You've gone from not wanting a funeral to not wanting a *burial*? Not wanting a place for her to *rest*?"

"No, I do—Nora, I do, maybe just...not *here*. Not practically in our back *yard*."

"She's our daughter, Pete," Nora said, and she caught that look on his face again. Disgust? Regret? "I want her close. Why wouldn't you? Why *don't* you?"

He chewed while she waited for an answer. He didn't have one and she knew why.

"Are you glad?" she asked, holding her hands very still.

He took another bite, stared at his plate.

"You are," she said.

"Stop."

"You *are*."

He looked at her and she looked back: new wrinkles creased his forehead, cut lines between his brows.

"*Nora*," he said. "Come on. That's not fair. Of course I'm not *happy* our baby died. Of course I'm not. But you know I never..."

He trailed off, shrugged like he'd run out of words.

The refrigerator hummed; the motor kicked on.

"Wanted kids," she finished for him.

"Yes! And *you* used to feel the same way!" he shouted, slapping his hand against the counter. Plates jumped; pizza crusts clattered to the floor. "We agreed on that, Nora. All those years ago. And *you* changed your mind. You. *I* never did." He pushed a greasy hand through his graying hair. "I just—I think our views on this are a little different."

She wiped her hands carefully on a paper napkin and swept aside her overgrown bangs.

"Our views," she repeated, voice ringing hollow. "On our dead daughter. Our dead baby daughter. Our views are different."

"I just meant—"

"No."

She couldn't look at him. She stood and walked away. Climbed the stairs, went to bed.

He slept on the couch.

Nora saw the stranger again at the funeral.

The priest muttered prayers over the tiny white coffin; a rectangular hole waited in the half-frozen earth. Nora looked up and there she was, at the back of the crowd that had come to gawk, standing near a tree alone.

Dark, fringed hair hid most of her face. What Nora could see was pale, sharp featured. She couldn't tell whether or not she was pretty.

That mattered to her, though she didn't know why.

"Hey!" Nora called. She rose from the cold metal folding chair someone had placed for her near the grave. The backs of her legs had gone numb, though she'd worn black wool dress pants to try to keep warm. "You!"

The priest stopped; everyone looked from him to Nora. Pete put a hand on her arm.

"Sit down," he said.

She glanced at him. At his red face. "But that woman. I—"

"Sit *down*," Pete hissed. "You're embarrassing us both."

Nora sat. But when the coffin was in the ground and the neighbors and coworkers and grief mongers broke apart to head to their cars, Nora looked for her—the woman who had been in her yard, who was now at her daughter's funeral, watching Pete, watching her. Nora scanned faces, hurried to check behind the oak trees that stood like silent giants all over the cemetery.

Pete came up behind her. He caught her elbow.

"I saw her," Nora said. "And I've seen her before. Do you know her?"

"Let's go," he said. He sounded tired. "Let's get you home."

Nora was tired too.

They went.

Early February. Still too cold to plant flowers on her baby's grave, but Nora could visit and sing her lullabies.

She came every day, in her winter coat or her raggedy blue cardigan or, once or twice, her robe.

Pete left in the mornings and came home most nights.

Valentine's Day, and the sun had barely risen in the sepia sky.

Nora crouched near her daughter's grave, drawing hearts in the powdery snow. They'd named her—*Nora* named her—Eden, after Pete's favorite grandmother. *Eden Renee*, not in cursive but almost, carved into the smooth marble surface.

The letters, to Nora, seemed so very small.

She hadn't wanted to add a date. Eden never took a breath. Why mark the day her baby died inside of her?

Another week passed. Maybe more.

Strange footprints in the cemetery.

Not the stomped muddy trail Nora left going between her backyard and her daughter's grave, but a trail leading away from Eden's headstone and winding into the oak trees.

Another visitor, then—not Pete. The prints were too small and besides, he wouldn't come.

Nora wiped her runny nose on the sleeve of her cardigan and followed them:

First down a narrow path...

Then around a tree...

Then around another...

Past a small mausoleum...

Up a sloping hill...

And finally past an overgrown, skeletal, thorn-studded rosebush.

She inhaled sharply. Frigid air burned her lungs.

In front of her stood a dozen little headstones—close together, some leaning—sheltered beneath the snow-weighted boughs of an evergreen tree.

Nora crouched down and read:

Alistair McKenna, June 1908.

William T. Grace, October 1914.

Julia, no last name, just the year: *1904.*

Samuel Albert, December 1912.

One, more weathered, simply marked *Eddy.*

It was a gravesite just for babies. A garden of heartbreak: seeds that never grew.

Nora traced their names with her finger, whispering as she did: *"I'm sorry, so sorry, you were loved, I'm sorry."*

Tears fell from her cheeks, disappeared in the snow.

For a long time, she stayed. Until dusk fell and her toes went numb inside her wet cloth sneakers.

She'd wanted to tell Pete all about it—the odd footprints and tiny headstones with their pitiful little names.

But when she walked into the house, he was speaking with someone on the phone. He saw Nora, whispered a few words, and ended the call.

She went upstairs.

"I spoke with your doctor," he told her in early March. "He agrees with my concerns. He prescribed some pills for you—just to take until you're feeling better. They'll be ready at the pharmacy this afternoon."

Pete stood by the sink, swallowing the last dregs of his morning coffee. He set the mug down too hard; Nora winced.

"Honey?" he said. "Did you hear me?"

She looked at him from her stool at the counter and scratched at a patch of eczema on her neck. She coughed. Cleared her throat. "I'm not sick."

"You are, Nora," he said. His eyes were soft, like they used to be. She thought about stepping closer, wrapping her arms around him, burying her face in his suit jacket. He reached out a hand. "In a way, you are. Postpartum—"

She stiffened. "I'm not sick," she said.

He let his hand drop to his side. "Please pick up the pills. Please," he said.

He hadn't begged her for anything in a long time.

"Okay," she said.

He called from his office later on to remind her. Nora heard a woman's voice in the background—a low, throaty laugh.

Did she have dark hair? Sharp cheekbones? Nora wondered.

"Remember," Pete said. "You promised. But don't drive, okay? Call a ride service."

Nora put on her blue cardigan and her cloth sneakers and did as she was told.

The lights in the pharmacy were too bright; they hummed above her as she made her way to the counter, squinting.

"Hello, Nora," said a voice behind her.

She turned.

It was Cheryl. From the parenting class Nora had taken at the community center in the fall. Cheryl held a fat infant in blue overalls. An older woman stood next to her, carrying a diaper bag printed with ducks.

"Hello," Nora said. But her voice came out rusty, failed by the end of the word.

Cheryl's face was locked in a cringe, but she might have been trying to smile. It reminded Nora of prying the lid off a can of paint. She wished she had a screwdriver, so she could help.

But the woman was talking.

"Listen. Nora, I meant to catch you at the funeral, but I didn't want to disturb you."

Nora looked at her. At her healthy little boy.

"I just wanted to—well I wanted to tell you how very sorry I am for your loss. How sorry we all are, I mean—me and the other ladies from our class."

Nora watched her hug her baby tighter to her chest as she said it; splay protective fingers across his back, grip his chubby thigh.

"No," Nora said, almost a whisper. "No."

"What?"

"No you're not. Not sorry. You're just glad it wasn't you."

Cheryl's mouth opened and closed.

Nora left them there and walked to the counter, hit the little silver bell. While she waited for the pharmacist, she glanced over her shoulder to see Cheryl and the other woman leave—heads close together, eyes darting.

They hadn't bought anything.

Late that night, lying in bed, Nora caught the sound of Pete's voice from downstairs: hushed tones and a laugh. The word *us* just a whisper.

She rolled over and closed her eyes.

But before she could fall asleep, she heard crying: a baby... No—*babies*, plural.

Babies crying in the night.

Her daughter was dead but her instincts were not; Nora threw the covers back and got out of bed, shoved her feet into slippers, pulled on her robe as she rushed down the hallway and spun toward the stairs.

At the bottom Pete stood rubbing his eyes.

"What are you doing, hon?" he asked. "Why are you up?"

Nora tried to push past him.

"I need to find them," she said. "I need to get to them."

He caught her arm. "What? Get to who, Nora?"

"Can't you hear them?"

"No. What do you hear?" His voice was patient. "I think you had a nightmare."

"They're crying, Pete, for God's sake, let me go!"

"Who is, Nora?"

"The babies!"

He let go, pulled his hand back like she'd scalded him. Gave her that look—disgust and pity, now with fear mixed in, too.

Nora didn't care. She could tell the cries were coming from outside.

She hit the back door at a run, fumbling with the lock and throwing it open. She leapt off the deck, flew through the yard and through the gate, was almost past the first row of headstones when Pete caught up and threw his arms around her waist.

They both went down, hitting the muddy slush with a *thwack*.

"Nora!" Pete said, crawling, then standing. "You can't *do* this!" He pulled her up, held her tight, trying to pull her toward the house. Her dirty wet robe dragged along the ground. "*Please! Please, stop. Stop this. Stop* it." Tears streaked his face.

Nora ignored them, ignored him, and reached out—toward the babies, the ones calling her. She knew where they were, she could find them, even in the dark—but Pete wouldn't let her. Wouldn't let go. And the cries got louder—they needed her *now*.

They hadn't had anyone's love for so long. Not until *she* found them.

Pete didn't understand.

"I have to get to them!" she said. "I have to."

The hiccupping cries she heard turned to wails, turned to shrieks.

She brought her elbow back in a quick, desperate jab, hitting Pete in the nose, catching him off guard. He dropped her to cover his face; blood leaked through his fingers.

She left him; she ran.

The babies cried louder.

Her chest ached. It would burst. They cried louder. She ran faster. But the world tilted sideways, and she fell.

It all went quiet. It all went dark.

She woke up the next morning in her bed, wearing a clean nightgown. Mud still streaked her calves and her feet were filthy. She coughed. Her temples throbbed.

She got up to use the bathroom, then burrowed back into bed. Pete came to the door and looked in—two black eyes, a white strip of medical tape across his nose.

Nora opened her mouth—to apologize, ask questions—but he beat her to it, speaking quietly.

"I counted your pills," he said. "You haven't taken any. You don't eat. When's the last time you took a shower? Brushed your teeth? All you do is sleep and when you're awake you're doing crazy shit, like running out at night in your slippers in the snow. You broke my fucking *nose*, Nora. You said you heard a baby crying. Enough is enough."

"I did!" she said. She was sure of it. "It was real."

"No, it wasn't!" Pete said, louder, harsher. "How could it be? *Crying*, Nora? The baby—she couldn't be crying." He locked eyes with her. "She's gone."

Nora sat up, yanked the covers to her chin. "Her name is Eden!" she yelled. "And it wasn't just her! It was all of them."

"I'm calling your doctor," he said, turning away. "I'm going to see if he'll come to the house."

"I know about her," she said to his back.

She watched him stop. Saw his fists clench. But he didn't say anything—just went downstairs. A moment later she heard him talking on the phone.

She coughed. Rolled over and closed her eyes.

The doctor came. Nora swallowed pills. Pete glowered behind him, arms crossed. The doctor left. Nora slept.

Pete made her swallow pills in front of him before he left for work the next day. She'd washed her face, pulled her hair back in a limp ponytail. She smiled, told him she felt better.

"Good," he said, but he didn't smile back. He picked up his briefcase. "I'll be home late. Make sure you eat something." Then he plucked his keys from the rack by the door and walked out.

Nora waited until his car had left the driveway, cleared their street, turned onto the main road. She found her blue cardigan in the kitchen and her sneakers in the hall; a coughing spasm took her when she leaned down to tie them. When it passed, she straightened up and hurried out the back door, across the yard and through the gate.

The cemetery looked the way it always did, which was a comfort to her.

Rows and rows of monuments in granite and marble and types of stone she couldn't name. Countless oak trees standing, a few pines here and there. Mausoleums squatting like gargoyles in the older sections. Pedestals topped with angels and cherubs. Rose and forsythia bushes waiting for spring.

She walked to Eden's grave and spent an hour with her. Then she visited the other babies. Her heart ached for them; alone for more than a century. She said each of their names so many times it sounded like a prayer.

When she visited them she sat on the ground—it wouldn't be right to sit on one of their gravestones. Then she'd tell them about the world, all that they'd missed. No—not all. She left out the ugly parts.

Nora was in the middle of describing Fred Astaire's dancing when she realized morning sun had turned into afternoon bluster. Cold rain came down, light at first, then harder, freezing halfway to become sleet.

Nora stood to leave, turned in the direction of the path that would take her home.

And there she was. The woman. The stranger. Drenched herself, and watching Nora from the shadows at the side of a mausoleum.

Had she *followed* Nora? Had she *been* following her?

"Hey!" Nora shouted.

The woman moved away, kept her hands in her pockets and ducked her head. She didn't hear Nora, or ignored her.

So Nora jumped up to tail her, but another coughing fit slowed her down. By the time she could stand, trying to run on numb feet, the woman was too far ahead—shoulders hunched, trudging. She disappeared through the break in the fence—the one leading to Nora's backyard.

It had to be her: Pete's woman on the side. Spying, wanting to catch a glimpse of the sad, used-up wife. How much did Pete tell her, Nora wondered? What did they share, aside from sex? Did Pete fuck this woman on his desk at work, the way he'd fucked Nora so many years ago? New company now, new desk. Same man.

The stranger was gone by the time Nora made it through the gate, wheezing. Her lungs ached from the effort; her shins throbbed.

But Nora saw her telltale footprints.

Her husband's girlfriend didn't know enough to cover her tracks. Or maybe she didn't care—it wasn't like Pete tried that hard to hide it.

Nora swept her hair out of her eyes and went inside, still thinking. Did Pete love this other woman? Did he still love *her*? Did Nora push him away or did he run?

And if she tried, could she make him run back, or was he too far gone?

When Pete got home—late, like he said, Nora was waiting up for him. She'd showered, shaved her legs, put on a little makeup. She even wore a nightgown he liked—mauve silk and black lace.

"What's all this?" he said. He put down his briefcase, shrugged his coat off and hung it up. "Are you… Do you feel okay?"

She walked to him and put her arms around his neck. She kissed his jawline and his earlobe, ran her tongue along his bottom lip.

But he put his hands on her waist and gently, so gently, pushed her away.

She stumbled back. Tears pooled in her eyes and spilled over.

"I just thought—" she said. "I wanted—"

"Wanted what?" Pete said, sounding tired, not mad. "To forget the past three months? Forget how sick you are? Just pretend it's all fine?"

"Yes," Nora whispered. She closed her eyes. Her throat hurt. "For a little while. Yes."

"Nora, I—"

She wanted him to say *I love you.*

"I can't."

She looked at him. His face was open and raw.

She wanted to smash it.

Instead she turned around, gathered up the hem of her nightgown so she wouldn't trip, and walked up the stairs.

Behind her, she heard him swear, grab his keys. The door opened and shut; his car drove away.

She shuffled down the hall and into her bedroom.

She tried to sleep.

An hour later, something woke her. A sound. Pete? But no—she could tell the house was empty.

He hadn't come home. She lay in the dark, listening.

A cry. Another.

They were calling her again.

No one to stop her, this time. No one to fight her back—tell her she imagined it, tell her she was sick.

"I'll be right there, sweethearts," she called. She got out of bed and pulled on her robe. Stuck her feet into slippers and ran down the stairs. "I'm coming." Through the kitchen. Out the back door. "Hang on, loves." Across the yard. "I'm coming."

Through the gate.

On and on.

She splashed through slick mud and standing water, her robe absorbing it like a sponge. The heavier it got, the heavier it dragged. Still she ran, ignoring the freezing air and her own shivering. Ignoring the pain in her chest, the cough locked in her throat that threatened to take her down.

She ran past Eden's quiet grave and down the path, into the older section of the cemetery.

When the little headstones came into view, the crying stopped.

They knew she was there. They cried for her and she came. Just like she was meant to. Just like mothers do.

"That's right, my darlings," she gasped, shuffling closer. "I'm here. It's alright. I've got you. I'm here."

She doubled over to cough and lost her balance, caught herself with a hand on Eddy's grave. She said his name. She said Eden's too. She said them all and then again.

She knelt down, entranced: the cemetery spread before her like an unfolded map. Moonlight cast the snow and ice in silver; melting puddles reflected its glow. Nora leaned over to look into one, to see the sky captured in a few drops of water.

But what she saw wasn't moon, wasn't stars.

It was the stranger. Pete's woman.

Her.

Dark hair hung like broken shutters. Cheekbones jutted from beneath shadowed eyes.

Nora cried out—pushed herself away, kicked at the puddle to shatter that face. Her back met cold stone; she found herself propped against Samuel's leaning grave marker.

Her chest heaved. She coughed. Her skin froze; her lungs burned.

She tried to breathe. She felt so tired. She pulled her robe tighter, but it did no good. She shivered and sweated, sweated and shivered.

She needed to rest here, just for a bit, or she'd never make it back to the house and to Pete.

But why would she want to? Around her, so quiet, barely there and then louder, she heard a lovely sound: the contented gurgles and sighs of her babies. One laughed. One cooed. Another blew a raspberry.

Nora smiled, let her head fall back.

There on the cold ground, she shivered and shivered and then she stopped. Her ragged breathing stilled. Her hand fell from her chest; dropped into muddy slush.

She didn't feel it. She didn't feel anything—never would again.

The babies hushed. The cemetery quieted.

The night stretched on.

ONE RED GLOVE

BY JONATHAN GENSLER

Swoosh.

Swoosh.

Swoosh.

The snow flies from the edges of your skis—it's a powder day like you've never experienced. Eighteen inches since lunch, the falling flakes so thick that the mountain is empty, not that a Tuesday in late February would have a crowd. Not at a small resort like this, so far off the beaten path.

But this is how you like it:

You.

The mountain.

A few hundred inches of bright white snow.

And then you see red.

You swoop in near the left treeline, and the splash of color is a gash on the washed-out green of the pines.

Is it…? No, it can't be.

You hear a faint cry, the warble of a wounded animal muffled by the wind and the sound of skis carving mountain snow.

You come to a hockey stop against a cat track into the trees—the red splash is a glove, caught on a small, spiky branch.

Small.

A lone bit of fabric in the shape of a hand.

Where is its partner? Who left it here?

The wind picks up, lifts the glove and blows the palm to the side, the sole finger held by the nail pointing to the wood.

The sharp cry again, farther into the trees than you can see, echoing. You know you could go on. You *should* in fact go on, head to the lift base and report this. Maybe if you wait for a minute, another skier—or if you're lucky, Ski Patrol—will head down the trail behind you. There aren't that many trails down on this side of the mountain. It isn't busy, but it isn't empty, either; at least it wasn't an hour or three earlier at the Peaks for lunch.

What time is it now?

The sun is setting. Maybe half hour until the lifts close. If you take off, and if someone *is* hurt, they could be out here all night. The snow will keep falling, and you'll never find this place again, even if you did make it down and back up again with a Patroller.

You know you have to help if you can.

It's the code of the mountain.

You hear the scream again, still muffled by the trees closing in around you, the snow swirling.

Mom! Wake up! Mom! Mom? The voice crumples in on itself, and the wind carries a sob to you.

Images flash in your mind: *Your own daughter, Amelia, flying down the mountain ahead of you. Missing a mogul, her skis skidding, she is going too fast, too close to the trees. She disappears beyond the crest, and her tiny voice fills your ears.* You're not alone after all. How could you forget you came here with your own daughter?

Her scream blends with the sobs in the here and now, the forever of the now, the endless driving snow of the now, you are here NOW, and you can do something different. Your skis are off, and you are stomping through the accumulating drifts under the trees, somewhat shallower here, and you are light on your feet, miraculously, gliding over the snow toward the screaming child, echoes of *Mom!* bouncing around you, off the pine branches, off the granite rock of the mountainside, the cliffs above the trees, pushing you forward.

You feel it. You can do something different. Help. The need to fix what has happened—*what has happened?*—overwhelms you and you break through the cover to the far side.

You see her.

The girl. Shaking someone, trying to wake them up. A shape, certainly not dressed for the weather. Is she even wearing a coat?

The snow around her legs is streaked bright red.

Red like the glove.

The glove in your hand. You hold it up in front of you: the red glove. Did you take it off the tree and bring it with you?

Hello? Young woman? She is no little girl, this screaming, crying, shouting young thing.

She glances up toward you through the snow. Scans the trees, as if she can't see you. Her eyes, so familiar. *Your* eyes. But not your eyes. A sharper shade of green.

Amelia's eyes.

"Amelia!" you bellow over the steadily increasing snowstorm. "Amelia! It's me!"

But she looks back down, tears streaming off her face. Amelia wears your coat for some reason. The woman Amelia is holding wears none.

Who is the woman on the ground? You are frozen in place, can't force yourself to move any closer. You can't understand why she isn't wearing her coat. You glance down and see the crooked shape of your daughter's arm.

You try one more time, and your voice grinds to a whisper. "Amelia..."

Behind you, more shouting. The *whoop whoop* of an emergency vehicle. "Hello! We saw the glove, is anyone there!?"

A man appears, wearing the Red Cross of emergency services. Amelia screams at him, "My mom! Help her!" Then, "Oh god, my arm..." ending with a whimper, and she clutches the tied-off tourniquet around her right forearm.

"Are you okay? Ma'am…" is the last thing you hear before the wind picks you up like you are nothing—and you *are* nothing—and wisps you away, away, and away.

You are with her. Holding her. You've splinted the break. You've stopped the bleeding with your own shirt. A compound fracture—oh god, how are you going to get out of this? There is so much blood. She is breathing. She is breathing, and the bleeding has stopped. But you are so cold. You've done all you can. How will anyone find you? The sun is going down. She is too cold. You give her your jacket for extra warmth and hold her.

You are alone. Amelia dreams in your arms. You scramble for any hint of warmth at all and find an old pair of gloves in her jacket pocket. As you stop breathing, one red glove is the last thing you see.

THANK YOU

Thank you for reading *The Hauntings Back Home* by Rebecca Cuthbert.

We appreciate your support of Undertaker Books, as well as all of the indie authors and small-press publishing houses.

Please leave Rebecca a review on Goodreads and/or Amazon.

ACKNOWLEDGMENTS

The person who gets the first thanks is the same one I love so much I tied my life to his. He is also the reason I jumped into the horror genre with both feet. Thank you, Joel, for everything you do to make my existence joyful and fun and funny every single day. Let's listen to a podcast.

Next, of course, is Jonathan Gensler, who wrote the foreword for this book and agreed to contribute his gem "One Red Glove" for the lucky thirteenth story. His writing is amazing, and if you haven't read his other work, check it out via *Cosmic Horror Monthly*, *OnSpec Magazine*, *Creepy Pod*, and other venues. For more, visit and subscribe to his newsletter, *The Modern Macabrist.*

To Beatrice Sheehan, thanks so much for allowing us to publish this poem. It's always special when we can claim the honor of being the first to showcase a debut author.

Big thanks to my publishing partners, D.L. Winchester and Cyan LeBlanc, at Undertaker Books. They made room for this collection when another small press shuttered, adding their editing and formatting talents as well. Thanks, guys.

Thank you to Ruth Anna Evans for the beautiful cover. It's perfect for these stories.

Thank you my writing mentors, Moaner Lawrence and Lindsay Merbaum. Those two and their workshops are responsible for so many of these stories—their creation *and* development. If folks get a chance to apply for Fright Club or join the Study Coven, I recommend it wholeheartedly.

Thank you to the generous authors who took time out of their busy schedules to read and blurb this collection: Christopher O'Halloran, Paul Jessup, Chloe York, Liam Burke, Lindsay Merbaum, Moaner Lawrence, JG Faherty, and Aimee Hardy.

Special thanks to Jen Griffin, who wrote an early review of the collection for *Horror Tree*. There are hundreds of titles vying for reviewers' attention, especially in ARC or galley form, and I appreciate so much that THE HAUNTINGS BACK HOME made the cut!

And finally, thank you to all the readers out there who love ghost stories as much as I do. Stay spooky, folks!

About Rebecca Cuthbert

Rebecca Cuthbert (she/her) writes dark fiction and poetry. She loves ghost stories, folklore, witchy women, gothic settings, and anything that involves nature getting revenge. Her titles include *In Memory of Exoskeletons* (poetry), *Creep This Way: How to Become a Horror Writer with 24 Tips to Get You Ghouling* (craft and memoir), *Self-Made Monsters* (stories and poems), *Down in the Dark Deep Where the Puddlers Dwell* (all-ages picture book), and *Six O'Clock House & Other Strange Tales* (stories). For more information, free stories, interviews and more, visit linktr.ee/rebeccacuthbertwrites.

About Jonathan Gensler

Jonathan Gensler (he/him) grew up in a haunted house in West Virginia and has stories in *Cosmic Horror Monthly*, *OnSpec Magazine*, and *Creepy Pod*, among other venues. An Army combat veteran, recovering entrepreneur, and Active Pro Member of the HWA, he lives and writes in the Rocky Mountains with his wife and three children. You can connect with him online at jonathangensler.com.

ABOUT BEATRICE SHEEHAN

Beatrice Sheehan lives in Western New York with her mom, dad, brother, and dog Leo. She enjoys reading, writing, and musical theater. This is her first publication.

READER ADVISORIES

Most of these stories have to do with death and grief. We hope these notes will help those who are sensitive to certain situations and subject matter. For specifics, see below:

"Downstairs at The Sabine" portrays death.

"The One That Got Away" features a young woman whose brother goes missing. Other townspeople are killed.

"Ghost in the Gas Station Bathroom" details an assault and stabbing.

"The Vines That Bind" hints at possible elder abuse and portrays death.

"Let the Black Dog In" explores grief in a symbolic way.

"Suffer with the Trees" hints at infidelity and portrays death.

"Ghost-Knocking" references death.

"Mrs. Anderson, Mrs. Anderson" features sexual situations, infidelity, terminal illness, and death.

"The Hole Had Always Been There" references death and portrays grief.

"Dead Man's Pie" has a graphic death scene in it.

"Restoring the Empire Review" portrays an attack on a woman

and arson, and references death.

"Rock-a-Bye" details pregnancy loss and grief, marital strife, possible infidelity, and death.

"One Red Glove" depicts an accident and death.

We hope you will enjoy these stories, but first and foremost, Undertaker Books wants its readers to take care of themselves and honor their own boundaries. Thank you!

If you are a fan of horror stories and tales,
you'll want to follow Undertaker Books.
We're bringing you stories to take to your grave.